M000097011

The Time Under Heaven

Laurinda Wallace

3-Mice Productions

Sierra Vista, AZ

THE TIME UNDER HEAVEN

© 2012 Laurinda Wallace

ISBN: 978-0-9854328-0-5

Cover Design by C.D. Davis

Cover image by Racheal Grazias

Author Photo by Jesaro Photography

Scripture quotations marked (NLT) are taken from the Holy Bible, New Living Translation, copyright © 1996, 2004, 2007 by Tyndale House Foundation. Used by permission of Tyndale House Publishers, Inc., Carol Stream, Illinois 60188. All rights reserved.

Scriptures taken from the Holy Bible, New International Version®, NIV®. Copyright © 1973, 1978, 1984, 2011 by Biblica, Inc.™ Used by permission of Zondervan. All rights reserved worldwide. www.zondervan.com.

ALL RIGHTS RESERVED

No part of this publication may be reproduced, stored in a retrieval system, or transmitted, in any form or by any means—electronic, mechanical, photocopying, recording, or otherwise—without prior written permission.

For information contact:

3-MICE PRODUCTIONS ◆ PO Box 415 ◆ Hereford, AZ 85615

This is a work of fiction. Any references to real events, businesses, organizations, and locales are intended only to give the fiction a sense of reality and authenticity. Any resemblance to actual persons, living or dead is coincidental.

The Time Under Heaven

Dedication

For my sisters, Amy and Yvonne

The Time Under Heaven

There is a time for everything,
A season for every activity under heaven.
A time to be born and a time to die.
A time to plant and a time to harvest.
A time to kill and a time to heal.
A time to tear down and a time to rebuild.
A time to cry and a time to laugh.
A time to grieve and a time to dance.
A time to scatter stones and a time to gather stones.
A time to embrace and a time to turn away.
A time to search and a time to lose.
A time to keep and a time to throw away.
A time to tear and a time to mend.
A time to be quiet and a time to speak up.
A time to love and a time to hate.
A time for war and a time for peace.

Ecclesiastes 3:1-8 NLT

1

Ruthanne sat on the rusty folding chair, picking at the corner of the worn manila file in her hands, watching the second hand on the large black wall clock make its circumference. The day was hot as always. Flies buzzed lazily in the air above her, and the sharp smell of disinfectant stung her nose. The large-paddled fan that moved the thick, humid air clicked steadily. A thin trickle of sweat rolled from her underarms and down the inside of her yellow cotton blouse. Her dark blue skirt clung to her legs. A crying child in the next room suddenly stopped, and the low murmur of conversation in Swahili increased in volume when the door to the examination room opened. The tall, American doctor stood smiling at the young African mother, who comforted the pudgy toddler on her shoulder. Her elegant, long face was adorned with red and white beads that draped her head and around her neck. The *shuka* she wore was a red geometric print. Ruthanne recognized her as one of the newest mothers who was attending the childcare class she taught on Tuesdays. She tried to remember their names. The names spun from the list she kept in her head. The little boy was Isaac, and the mother's name was Somoine. She pulled a small spiral notebook from her raffia tote bag and quickly wrote the names down on her prayer list.

"Asante, doctor. Asante," Somoine said gratefully, repositioning the little boy, who wrapped his fat arms tightly around his mother's neck. Tears were still drying on his cheeks. The woman's large hoop earrings clattered against the beads.

The doctor patted Isaac's head and nodded. He turned toward the waiting area, caught Ruthanne's eye, and motioned for her. She stood, willing her legs to move forward. She quickly pulled the damp fabric from the back of her thighs as she stepped toward the doctor's office.

"Good morning, Miss Carroll," the doctor said pleasantly. "Or should I say Jambo?"

"Either one will do." She smiled, handing him the file now moist with perspiration from her hands.

"The test results?"

She nodded. She already knew what the folder contained. The MRI report was clear enough for her to understand. Ruthanne ran her hands across her hips, trying to dry them on the skirt's coarse cotton fabric. Dr. Hawkes sat at a dented gunmetal gray desk that must have been new around World War II or earlier. She sat on a hard wooden chair near the whitewashed cement block wall, trying not to watch the young doctor read the paperwork. Behind him, mountains rose up like a fortress beyond the smudged glass of the office window. Psalm 121 ran through her head. "I lift up my eyes to the hills—where does my help come from?"

"Where was help coming from?" she wondered. She took a deep breath and let it out slowly, trying to steady her thoughts.

Dr. Hawkes was new to the Maasai village in the Rift Valley area. The health clinic had been empty for a year, and now the energetic, brown-haired and brown-eyed doctor was trying to get all the children vaccinated and develop a regular schedule of care for the area. She heard the new nurse, recently arrived from Nairobi, speaking to more patients in the outer office, most of them with crying children. The doctor seemed oblivious to the noise just outside the door. A fly crawled across the top of the desk, and without warning he slammed it with a flyswatter that must have lain across his knees. He smiled boyishly and shut the file. She couldn't help but snicker at his smile of satisfaction.

"It's not a good report, but you probably already realize that," he said matter-of-factly. His grin had disappeared, and the timbre of his voice matched the seriousness of the papers inside the folder.

"I know," she answered softly, intertwining her fingers.

"You'll need surgery, and there are treatments, but I'd recommend that you go back to the States for them. You'll need the support of friends and family. And the best medical care—"

"My friends and family are here," she interrupted. "I haven't been back in five years. Besides, my work is here. I need to finish what I've started. These people need me."

6

"I totally understand that. The Maasai are wonderful people. But, if you're going to have a chance, a real chance to beat this, you need to go home. That will be my recommendation to the mission board too."

"What if I refuse treatment? What can I expect? How long..." Her energy was suddenly sapped, and the now familiar pain was like a hot pulse in her gut.

The intense dark eyes of the doctor bored into hers, and he sighed. Leaning back in the squeaky armless desk chair, he pushed his long fingers against the edge of the desktop.

"Six months, tops, Miss Carroll," he said finally. "I can't promise I can manage your pain or even provide nursing care. And you will need care. If you get treatment in the next few weeks, you have a real shot at two or three years, maybe more."

Ruthanne couldn't meet his penetrating gaze any longer. Her eyes shifted to the small wooden cross that hung a little crookedly on the wall near the window. She didn't want to go back to the States. There wasn't much there for her. Her sisters had their own lives. An occasional email was their only communication. Their parents were gone. Her supporting churches would expect slideshows and endless presentations. She didn't have the energy for it right now. The demands and the pace of American culture would suck her dry within weeks. There had to be other options. She'd go to Nairobi for treatment, and then she'd be back. She wouldn't have to leave.

"I'll have to think about it," she said, licking her dry lips. "And of course, I'll pray about it."

"Of course. But don't take too long. You have a small window of real opportunity. If you get the right treatment, you may be able to finish your project here. It'll wait for you."

"That project can't wait. The children need it too badly."

"As I said, it's a small window, Miss Carroll. After that..." He stood and handed her the file. "I'll pray you make the right decision." John Hawkes extended his right hand, and she gripped his strong hand with matching strength.

"Thank you, doctor. God has never failed me." She forced herself to smile. But it seemed she had failed God time and time again. She couldn't leave this project unfinished. It was the work He had given her. Tucking the file under her arm, she fled through a rear exit, avoiding the women and children in the waiting room who knew her so well. She needed some time alone and that was difficult, if not impossible.

She walked quickly down the path to her home at the edge of a grove of acacia trees. A slight breeze stirred through their thorny branches. The smell of cattle dung hung in the air. The large grazing area for the cattle called a *kraal* was not far from the path. Goats bleated in the distance. Young boys watched over the cows and goats as they grazed on stiff grasses. Ever wary of predators, they kept a sharp watch for lions or hyenas who might dare to come close to the village for an easy meal. The boys sang a rhythmic chant that soothed her mind. Ruthanne couldn't imagine leaving here. It broke her heart every time she left on furlough. The school building was so close to completion, and she'd fought hard to get it for these hurting people. She had to see it to completion. There was no one else. Dr. Hawkes didn't have the time. The mission had no one to send. She was the project manager, grant writer, and teacher. The whole village was counting on her. The children were especially counting on her. They would finally have real classrooms. Desks, blackboards, books, even computers. Every day, boys and girls from preschool to junior high age greeted her on the way to the church, dancing around her, little ones tugging at her skirt, excitedly asking when it would all arrive. There were grants to be monitored and regulations to be met. The village elders had experienced so many disappointments from the government and other agencies. If she left the school unfinished, it would never happen. After so many years of pleading, debating, and finally succeeding, this *had* to happen.

Her small, round house made from traditional building materials of mud, sticks, and cow dung stood quiet. Hellen, her housekeeper was not there. Ruthanne sighed gratefully. If she just had a few minutes to herself before someone came to the door. She needed to pray, to clear her mind, and breathe. A thick blanket was suspended on a wire that ran the width of the house at the back. It was the wall that gave her privacy for the small sleeping area. The cot was made up neatly.

Her worn, black leather-bound Bible lay on the small carved table at the head of the cot. A kerosene lamp sat next to it. She pulled the blanket further along the wire to create a greater sense of isolation. Privacy was a luxury here. It seemed that an endless stream of needs was always at the door. Each one was important and immediate whether it was food, a disagreement that needed mediation, or a sick child, Ruthanne was always the first one the women came to see.

She looked into the old, chipped mirror that hung precariously over the small chest of drawers and took stock of her appearance. She didn't look sick. Her short, gray hair was wavy and cut close to her face. Her brown eyes, flecked with bits of gray, were clear, but dark circles puddled under them. The long bus ride from Nairobi to the large village of Asiri, and then jolting Land Rover ride to Kakuta must explain her fatigue. There were some lines, now etching deeper into her face, but she had turned 50 only weeks ago. She had earned them honestly. Her skin was dark brown, sprinkled with a few freckles on her arms that were strong from manual labor. She had lost weight though. The skirt and blouse hung loosely on her frame. She could hear her grandmother's voice admonishing her to eat and get some meat on her bones. She had always been a little thin, much to her sister Elizabeth's dismay, but this was different. Weight had slid from her body like water running off the roof in the rainy season in the last few weeks. She was sick. She tried to mouth the words, "I have cancer," but they stuck in her throat.

2

Melody pulled into her driveway, disgusted that the yard hadn't been mowed and the trash bag still lay on the front steps. With all the rain they'd had in June, the grass needed mowing twice a week. Everyone else in the cookie-cutter neighborhood with 70s-style, raised ranch tract homes seemed to manage it. What did Dennis do all day? He was laid off, yet he couldn't get his lazy backside off the couch and away from his beer long enough to do one simple thing. His pickup was in the side yard, so he must be home. She slammed the car door angrily and hauled two heavy bags of groceries into the house. She stumbled up crumbling cement steps to the kitchen. The steps were another project he'd never gotten to. The landlord had promised a hundred dollars off the rent if Dennis would fix them. Someone was going to break a leg or a neck on them. It would probably be her neck. Melody tossed the car keys into a wooden bowl on the kitchen counter and plopped the bags alongside.

"Hey there, beautiful," Dennis said. He sauntered into the kitchen from the living room with a can of beer in his hand and leaned against the counter.

She could tell he'd had way more than one if he was calling her beautiful. Most of the time, he didn't notice if she were dead or alive. If supper was on the table at the right time, he was happy. If she took care of everything, so he didn't have to lift a finger, all was right in Dennis' world. Melody put away the groceries while her husband grabbed the bag of chips she'd just bought and headed for the couch in the living room.

"When's supper going to be ready?" he called back to her.

"When the lawn is mowed," she answered sharply.

"What's that supposed to mean?" His voice took on an edge that Melody hated. He'd been so handsome and charming when they'd eloped almost 24 years ago. His dirty blond hair had been a little long, and his handsome face with its strong features had won her heart. He had been dangerously charming at 20 and confident about everything. She'd fought with her parents to see him many times. She'd snuck out after everyone was in bed when their answer had been "no." She remembered her father's stern, impassive face when she announced they were married. He'd simply said, "You've made your bed and now you'll have to lie in it." He'd stalked away to his inner sanctum to continue working on a sermon. Her mother had stroked her hair and told Dennis to take care of his wife. Melody still saw her mother's unshed tears, bright in her blue eyes. She sighed and leaned against the counter.

Her father had been right about Dennis. He hadn't amounted to anything. He was now an occasionally employed electrician, who was going to seed. The Reverend Carroll had also objected to Dennis' lack of Christianity and church attendance. He'd disapproved of her deficiency in that department too. If he were still alive, her father would probably tell her she was reaping what she'd sowed.

"It means I'll make supper when you've mowed the lawn Dennis. What did you do all day?"

"Get off my back. I had things to do. I'll mow tomorrow, your highness. Get me another beer. The ball game is on."

"Get it yourself. I'm busy."

She heard him mumble and turn up the volume on the TV. She sat down in a wobbly chair at the cheap kitchen table in front of the window. Her feet were killing her. She rubbed her tight, aching calves and took off the worn support shoes. She really needed a new pair, but she hoped she could make them last for two more paychecks. The rent was due next week, and so was the truck payment. Dennis' unemployment benefits barely covered his truck payment, and she'd have to scrape together enough to pay the landlord. He'd already given them an extension. There wouldn't be another one. She was sure of that. Melody stretched her legs out, flexing her toes. She rested them on the facing chair and looked out the window. A cigarette would have been good right now, but she'd given them up a month ago trying to save a few more dollars. A friend at the nursing home had given her some leftover nicotine patches, and somehow she'd been able to quit. Well, mostly anyway. She'd bummed a cigarette at break time a week ago, but so far this week she was good. She rested her head in her hands, elbows bent on the cool, yellow Formica tabletop, staring at the kids next door who were running through a lawn sprinkler. Summertime was supposed to be fun.

The squeals of laughter from the kids in the next yard confirmed that. Life wasn't fun anymore. There had been some good years at the beginning with Dennis, but now there were only piles of bills, car repairs, and fighting. There weren't even any kids, but that was her fault. Three miscarriages, and then a hysterectomy had taken care of that. Having kids could have made things better. Dennis might have been more responsible, had more ambition. They'd never been a real family. That was another wound her father had liberally rubbed salt into. Their union hadn't been blessed by God. Well, maybe it hadn't, but she'd proved to Daddy that her commitment to the marriage was up to his standard.

She leaned back in the chair, ruffling her short blond hair that framed her fine features. A pert nose, pouty mouth, and a voluptuous figure had gotten her lots of attention from the boys in high school, and especially Dennis. Now at 42, she felt bone-tired every night and didn't have time to care about what she looked like. There were too many other worries.

Stacy Mullen, mother of the slew of kids next door, turned off the water to the sprinkler. Towels were handed out, and the laughter faded as a lawn mower roared into action further up the street. The steady slap of the Mullen's screen door and empty yard signaled it was suppertime. She turned her gaze back to the kitchen that smelled of stale beer and bacon grease. Beer cans were piled on the counter. He couldn't even put them in the trash. She grumbled to herself and cleared the counter. Maybe she'd make some eggs, but then he'd want her to make him something else.

She settled on a peanut butter sandwich and took it along with a can of diet Coke to the small patio at the back of the house. A light breeze came through the yard from the west. It suddenly reminded her of the breezes at Cape Cod from summer vacations long ago. She and her sisters traipsed along the shore, collecting shells, and watching the waves. Their mother kept watch from a lounge chair, sketching them on a large pad of paper. They loved to examine the drawings at the end of the day. Mama was able to catch a look or a feeling in her pencil sketches that fascinated them all. Their father rarely joined them, preferring to spend his time in Bible study at the family cottage. Mama's family cottage. At least at the beach, they could run and shout without being shushed and told to be quiet because Daddy was studying. Sometimes they danced in the foamy, cold water that lapped at the beach, pretending to be fairies or ballerinas. The bite of salt air, the grit of the sand between her toes, and the cry of gulls overhead—all just memories. Melody and Dennis hadn't taken a vacation in years. There was never any money for that. Vacation for her husband was a case of beer and non-stop ESPN.

She finished the last of the peanut butter sandwich, brushing crumbs from her light blue uniform smock.

Dennis was sound asleep on the couch, the baseball game blaring. She had to work an early shift tomorrow. She clicked off the TV and dragged her weary body up the stairs to take a shower. Maybe she should finally leave him. The marriage wasn't going to change. She'd wanted it to change, and she'd tried to make it change. She'd loved him once. Then she stayed to prove her father wrong about them. But now...what reason was there? Her sister, Elizabeth had given her opinion more than once about that. They should go to counseling, they should try harder, or they should go to church. Elizabeth could sure preach like Daddy. It was a little scary at times. Lately though, she'd mentioned that Melody ought to get on with her own life. Maybe she should.

The hot water of the shower eased the tension in her neck and back. Lifting patients all day long made her back ache constantly. How many more years of this could she take? She should have gotten her RN and moved into administration. Paperwork was boring, but it didn't weigh 240 pounds, like the stroke patient she'd cared for this afternoon. A change would be good, with or without Dennis. If only Ruthanne was around to talk to. What would she say about the sad state of her little sister's life? She might get another sermon. She slipped under the sheets and fell into a dreamless sleep.

3

The breakfast table was cleared. Elizabeth stood rinsing dishes before loading the dishwasher, enjoying the view from the kitchen window. The iris and peonies punctuated the lower garden with bold purples and pinks against the soft blue delphiniums. The profuse magenta peonies were bent low, the weighty blooms scarcely off the ground. She'd have to stake them today. Happily her favorite, the Lincoln rosebush, was heavily budded. She leaned against the sink, anticipating the fragrance that would drift into the house when the large buds opened. She'd have to get her crystal vase from the cupboard, so it would be ready for the first bouquet.

Elizabeth put the last of the breakfast dishes in the dishwasher and wiped her hands on the kitchen towel. The house was quiet now that Tom had left for work. It wouldn't be for long though. Sonya, her daughter-in-law, would drop off three very busy little people in less than an hour. The 18-month-old twins Emma and Clara and their four-year-old brother Matthew would descend upon her solitude with giggling and hugs. She smiled. Grandchildren were the best thing that could have happened at this time in her life. Tom was so absorbed in his career. As the HR director of a small technology startup, that after just five years employed over 200 people, his focus wasn't at home. Now that their two children were out of the house, life was too quiet.

Paul, their oldest, was 28 and had married Sonya five years ago. Fortunately, they still lived in town and were only three blocks from Elizabeth and Tom. It still amazed Elizabeth that her own children had grown up so quickly. She felt her chest tighten when she thought about Corinne. She could just imagine what her father, the rigid and austere pastor, would say about his granddaughter if he were still alive.

Her bright and lovely daughter had quit college at Christmas break. Corinne had been a sophomore at the University of Rochester, still trying to find her major. She came home Christmas week, declaring she was in love with Trevor and was traveling the world with...this...this young man, or boy as Tom called him. She shut her eyes, remembering the ugly quarrel and the night Corinne stormed out. She had never seen Tom so angry. Her gentle and usually cool-headed husband disappeared in the heat of the argument. He had cut off any financial support in January, and it was now June. They hadn't heard from her since the end of January. Elizabeth prayed constantly that Corinne would just come home. She would ask no questions, and she wouldn't let Tom say a word either. They would just give the biggest party Sheffield had ever seen. So far, God hadn't seen fit to answer her prayers.

The doorbell rang brightly, breaking into her daydream. The threesome tumbled through the door, laughing. The twins were clutching Raggedy Ann dolls she'd made for their first birthday, and Matthew had his arms wrapped around his favorite truck. Kisses and hugs were given and received, and then they headed for the toy box in the family room. Sonya looked tired and out of sorts.

"Are you feeling all right?" Elizabeth asked.

"I'm OK. I didn't get much sleep last night. Matthew had a bad dream and got in bed with us. Then the alarm goes off so early for Paul to get up."

Elizabeth smiled, remembering many a sleepless night herself. "Why don't you leave the kids with me and get in an afternoon nap?"

"Are you sure? A nap would be great." Sonya's face brightened at the possibility.

"I'm sure. They'll go down for naps by one o'clock anyway. Pick them up at three or four. It'll be fine."

"Thanks, Elizabeth. I'll take you up on that offer. I'll just leave without goodbyes today. The girls are having a little separation anxiety lately."

"Go on. They'll be fine."

Elizabeth watched Sonya through the front window back the minivan out of the blacktopped driveway. She let the curtain fall back into place.

"Grandma, she took my truck." A tearful dark-haired Matthew sniffled, tugging at her shirt. Clara stood defiantly with a thumb in her mouth, clutching the coveted pickup truck. Emma was already pushing a stepstool to the island, bent on reaching the package of graham crackers and the Sippy cups that stood neatly in a row. The day wasn't going to be dull at all.

Her grandchildren were finally napping when she sat down at the laptop in Tom's study. She checked email several times a day, hoping that Corinne would finally contact them. She scrolled quickly through the new email. Nothing. A lump filled her throat, and tears threatened to spill over. She cleared her throat and blew her nose. Where was Corinne? Was she all right? Was she even alive? The questions were like swarming bees. Elizabeth gripped the edge of the computer desk angrily. If only Tom hadn't lost his temper. If only Corinne had been reasonable. If only she'd said something brilliant to stop the argument. If only God would answer her desperate prayers. If only. She shut down the computer and leaned back in the desk chair. She watched the pendulum on the antique Seth Thomas wall clock swing gently back and forth. She smiled suddenly, thinking it sounded like Tom's steady heartbeat when she laid her head on his chest. It was a comforting sound, but it had been a long while since she'd listened to her husband's heart.

Elizabeth was picking up the last of the toys when she heard a vehicle pulling into the driveway. Matthew ran to the front window and announced his mother's arrival. The twins weren't far behind, yelling "Mommy, Mommy" in unison. Sonya looked a little more rested when she came through the door. Her long honey-blond hair was swept back in a barrette.

"Ready to go, guys?" she asked the trio clamoring for her attention.

"Yes, Mommy. Let's go. Can we go to the store for ice cream?" Matthew clutched his truck and pulled on his mother's T-shirt.

"We're not getting ice cream. It'll ruin your supper, Matthew."

The little boy's dark brown eyes showed disappointment, and his lower lip jutted in a partial pout.

"Please, Mommy. I'll eat my supper."

Anna and Clara were already back at the toy box, pulling out blocks and scattering them over the hardwood floor.

"Girls. Let's go. Tell Grandma goodbye," Sonya said firmly. "And put the blocks away."

"Don't worry about that. I'll get them. Come on, girls. Time to go home with Mommy." Elizabeth herded the petite toddlers with curly dark blond hair toward the door. She scooped up Anna and received a sloppy kiss, while Clara pressed her mouth firmly shut and squirmed to get down.

"Thanks for taking them. The nap was good, and I was able to get a lasagna in the oven. Now let's hope Paul gets out of Rochester without any traffic jams or accidents tonight."

"Traffic is always horrible on the 490. Tom hates the drive anymore. Are you working again this week?"

"No. I'm finished with the agent's loss project, so I don't need to go back until next week. They have some new insurance software that I have to learn, so I might work three or four days. Will that be OK?"

"I'm always happy to have them. I'll help you get them in the car seats."

She stood on the sidewalk and waved to the little hands that appeared in the minivan's windows. The house was once again quiet, and she'd have to think about what to make for dinner tonight. Tom wouldn't be home until 6:00 or 6:30, so there was plenty of time. The phone was ringing when she opened the front door. The caller ID told her it was Melody. For a second, she was tempted not to answer. Melody was always in a predicament of some sort. If it wasn't finances, it was her marriage or her job. Elizabeth took a deep breath and said, "Hello."

"Hi, Beth. It's Mel."

"How are you?" She almost bit her tongue. She really didn't want to know, but the question was so automatic.

"OK. You know, for what we're going through right now."

Elizabeth groaned inwardly. She could hardly wait for the explanation.

"Has Dennis found a job yet?" This was usually Melody's biggest problem, so she might as well find out now.

"No. There just isn't any work out there right now. He's waiting to hear on a couple of interviews, though." There was a defensive tone in her sister's voice. She had no idea why Melody continued to protect her good-for-nothing husband. Elizabeth doubted there had been any interviews.

"I know things are tough for construction workers. I hope he'll get a job soon," she tried to sound conciliatory.

"He'll probably hear something in a week or two."

There was a pause, which signaled that Melody was probably going to ask for some money "to tide them over." Tom had put his foot down after the last loan to cover their auto insurance. He'd be livid if she caved in and wrote them another check.

"Beth, I was well, hoping you could lend me a little bit to..."

Elizabeth quickly cut her sister off. "Sorry, Melody. We can't help this time. I'm afraid the well is really dry."

"Oh," Melody said slowly. It was the first time Elizabeth had ever said a flat-out "no."

"It's not much, Beth. I really need new shoes for work. Mine are falling apart. My legs and feet are killing me. It's just until I get the next paycheck."

The sugary wheedling tone was classic Melody, and Elizabeth couldn't resist. Melody was her sister, and she had to help her. Tom had told her to stop enabling Mel's behavior, but how could she? Melody would always need help. That's the way it was.

"How much?"

"Eighty dollars. I promise I'll pay it back when..."

"Don't worry about it. I'll come over and drop it off. Are you home?" She was already disgusted with herself.

It was a good thing she had an emergency stash of cash. She wouldn't have to explain a check to Tom.

"I'm home. Dennis isn't here right now."

Elizabeth unclenched her jaw. At least she wouldn't have to face her brother-in-law. Every time she saw the man, she wanted to slap him for treating her sister so badly. Maybe they deserved each other. Tom certainly felt that way. Melody had always rebelled against making any rational decisions when it came to Dennis.

"All right. I'll be over in a few minutes."

"Thanks, Beth. I really appreciate this."

Elizabeth counted the money from the roll she kept in the jewelry box and shoved it in her wallet. Twenty minutes later, she pulled up in front of her sister's dilapidated rental house. The grass in the unkempt yard had to be three or four inches higher than any of the neighbors. The brackets on the flower boxes under the two front windows were rusted and had pulled away from the siding. Faded silk poinsettias along with a few sprigs of ratty plastic holly were stuck in them. What a mess! The house needed a coat of paint, too. Mama had always shaken her head at Melody's circumstances. She remembered the night that the phone call had come from her father about Melody's elopement. It was the first time she'd ever heard a tremor in his voice. The whole situation was hopeless, but she couldn't let her little sister go without the shoes she needed. Melody was on her feet all day long as a LPN at the nursing home. Even if Tom was right, she couldn't deny her own flesh and blood. It was the same with Corinne. She'd spend their life savings to get her back and never regret it.

Melody was struggling to pull the rope starter on the push mower. She stood and brushed the hair from her eyes and smiled at Elizabeth. Melody probably had the most powerful smile Elizabeth had ever seen. It had gotten her out of plenty of scrapes over the years. Their father was even charmed to a certain degree by it and was quick to blame Elizabeth and Ruthanne for not watching Melody properly or setting a bad example. Melody's face showed signs of deep fatigue that Elizabeth hadn't seen before. She must not be sleeping well, or maybe things were worse with Dennis. She was determined not to ask.

"Beth, thanks for coming over so fast. I know I shouldn't have asked, but I...I really need the shoes." Melody's voice trembled; her eyes were red and swollen. The shorts and tank top she wore must be size four. Where Melody had gotten her figure was still a mystery. Women on the Carroll side of the family tended to be tall and shapeless, and women on Erickson side were short and plump. Unfortunately, she took after their mother's side of the family. She hadn't seen a single-digit clothing size since grade school.

"It's all right, Mel. If you need the shoes, I'm happy to help. You're the bread winner right now." Elizabeth fought to keep her voice steady and gracious. The last thing she wanted was some emotional scene in her sister's front yard. She pulled the money from her wallet and handed it to Melody. "I've really got to go. Make sure you get those shoes."

"I will," Melody said, hugging her. She smelled of cigarette smoke and bug repellent.

Elizabeth watched her sister stuff the bills into the pocket of her denim shorts. She waved to Melody as she pulled back into the street. Melody smiled, returning the wave, then bent to pull the rope starter on the lawnmower again.

4

"I think it's the best for you and for the mission," Stephen Kauffman said with authority and finality in his voice. He was at least ten years younger than Ruthanne, and his wife, Megan, who was about her husband's age, sat quietly at the table, nodding in agreement. The couple had arrived mid-morning in a beat-up Land Rover, dusty and hot from the long ride from the outskirts of Nairobi. "Besides, you need a partner here as a single woman. It's been a year since Janine went home, and you're 18 months overdue for a furlough."

Ruthanne sat patiently, trying not to fidget and biting her tongue for fear she'd say something uncharitable. Stephen was a good director, one of the best she'd had over the years in Kenya. She knew he thought the decision was really the best for everyone. She remained unconvinced. The Lord needed her here, and she was determined to stick it out, no matter what the cost. Wasn't that what it was all about? She'd enjoyed working with Janine, but the solitary life here was much more pleasant. Surely the mission board must understand the urgency of the work.

"I understand why you'd say that," she began doggedly. "But I believe I can get the treatment I need in Nairobi. I can come back in a few weeks, and continue the school project. We're so close, Stephen. So close. It needs to be finished, and finished well. No one knows the people or the local system like I do. We're weeks ahead of where anyone else would be." She tried to check the passion in her voice. She didn't want to seem overwrought, just logical and practical.

The curly chestnut-haired, blue-eyed man pressed his hands against the edge of the rough-hewn table, working his jaw. Ruthanne knew she was pressing him a bit too hard. They'd already gone over that option a half hour ago.

"You're right," he responded after a few seconds of silence. "The people respect you and they want the school finished too. That's not the point, and I think you realize that."

"Ruth," his wife interjected, "you can always come back here after you get well in the States. You won't lose your place and the people love you so much. Just get well."

Megan Kauffman leaned across the table and placed her cool, white hands over Ruthanne's large, tanned ones. Ruthanne drew back, startled by physical contact. Never one for emotional displays, the last few weeks of humiliating tests had left her wanting to cocoon herself from any human contact. The Maasai women were naturally demonstrative, which had always been uncomfortable, but she'd gotten used to it. Now, she just wanted to be left alone. No more tests, surgery, or whatever else they wanted to do to her. God would give her the health she needed. Her life in the end was of no consequence, but she couldn't fail Him or the people she had grown to love so intensely.

The director's wife looked hurt when Ruthanne drew her hands back and wrapped them around her mid-section.

"I'm sorry, Megan. It's just...so much to deal with right now," Ruthanne said hastily, trying to make amends. From the stony look on the director's face, it was time to propose some sort of compromise. Stephen had the authority to send her back today, and she couldn't risk it. She plunged into what she believed to be a satisfactory solution for her and the mission.

"In another month or six weeks, the school will be finished. Then I can think about treatment in the States. The hospitals in Nairobi are perfectly capable of doing the hysterectomy. I could be back here in two weeks, and then when it's complete, I can make arrangements to go to the States for follow-up treatment. If you're available for two or three weeks, Stephen, you could oversee the building until I get back."

It really wasn't a fair compromise. She knew Stephen and Megan were planning to fly back to England in just a few weeks to reunite with their son and daughter, who were in school there. Megan's family was from a suburb in London, and the two teens lived with grandparents most of the year. It was, however, her

Gideon fleece she was throwing on the ground to see if God really wanted her to go or stay. If Stephen promised to continue the building project, she could get the surgery over with. If not, then she'd stay until the computers were loaded with software and the desks were in place, ready for students, even if she had to leave the mission.

A look of astonishment came over Megan Kauffman's face, and she gasped. The woman, a brunette who kept her pale complexion even in the intense African sun, became paler still. She was obviously thinking of her children. Who would think about the children of this village then? Sacrifices must be made.

The director looked her squarely in the eye and said without hesitation, "Of course, I'll stay. You need to get your health issues under control. If you'll pack, you can go back to Nairobi with Megan. But you'll have to go back to the States after the surgery. The mission board was quite definite about that. I'll stay here until the school is finished, and if the doctors permit, you can check up on me before you leave." He gave her a tight smile and avoided his wife's questioning eyes. "Dr. Hawkes tells me he has an extra bedroom at the clinic."

Her bluff had been called. She had been so sure he'd refuse. The confidence she'd had in her decision to stay was on shaky ground. Megan dug her nails into her husband's arm and looked pleadingly at him. He smiled and patted her hand.

"Why don't you go see Dr. Hawkes about getting your records, while Megan and I sort out our travel plans?" His voice couldn't have been more calm or mollifying. It was infuriating.

"You'll really stay here while I'm away? And I will come back here to finish as soon as they release me, correct?" She was leaving nothing to interpretation. Stephen Kauffman would have to keep every word, every jot and tittle to satisfy her. Her voice was a little sharper than she'd planned. She smiled to take the edge off her words.

"Absolutely. So, the sooner you have the surgery and set up any follow-up treatment, the sooner you'll return. Knowing you, it won't be long before you'll be on a plane back to Kenya. Is that a deal?" The stocky man stood, picking up his day planner and broad-brimmed straw cowboy hat.

Negotiations were over, and Ruthanne was now in a corner. Of course she'd have to agree to go. Nairobi was never the best option for chemo or radiation treatment. She just didn't want to contemplate being helpless and sick. Relying on others wasn't her forte. She swallowed what was left of her pride and nodded.

"I'll go," she said simply.

It was obvious that Stephen had primed the pump with Dr. Hawkes, who greeted her with arrangements for her surgery in a week's time. The handsome doctor seemed pleased with himself when she walked away with a new file folder filled with her test results and previous health history. Why was the Lord sending her away? He had the power to heal her. She firmly believed that, but the pain inside told her that there was no healing at the moment.

The pastor's wife, Esther Mitala, met her on the path back to the *kraal*. When Ruthanne reluctantly told her she must go to the United States, the woman's face fell, and tears began to flow. The heavy workload of the Maasai pastor and his wife was shared with Ruthanne alone.

The small congregation of 25 was new to the faith and struggling. The old ways were deeply ingrained, and the way of the Savior was only beginning to affect their lives. Between discipleship classes with women, childcare classes with young mothers, and managing the building project, there were never enough hours in the day. She was also working with a new organization called Sky Blue for fair trade crafts, so the women could make their own money. Esther was learning how to write music and lead a choir with the help of the mission's ethnomusicologist who came every two or three months. She was also teaching a women's Sunday School class, visiting church members with her husband, and raising three children. Neither one of them could squeeze another thing into their schedules.

Now that the dry season was coming, most of the village would move further south for better grazing. The cattle, which were the heart of Maasai culture, must eat so that the Maasai could eat. Some of the village would remain and tend small gardens, which was new to the thinking of the semi-nomadic warrior tribe. The warriors were without battles, except when tourists arrived. They dressed in full garb to impress awed Europeans and Americans, who took pictures as fast as camera shutters allowed. When the rain returned, so would the cattle and the rest of the village. The proud men were reduced to cattle herding and occasionally killing a lion, for which they were likely to be punished by the government. Many of the church members would stay throughout the summer. Worship and Bible study must go on.

The women wept and prayed. There was no time for good byes elsewhere. The other women wouldn't understand, although Esther had promised to do her best to explain the situation. Everything seemed to be spinning out of control. She clenched her fists, flexing her fingers and digging them into her palms. The hot wind that rushed through the tall grasses dried her tears before they dripped from her chin.

After breakfast and tearful devotions with Hellen the next morning, Ruthanne climbed into the Land Rover with Megan and their driver. Many women from the church had gathered around her to say goodbye. Departures were never simple, and finally she'd torn herself away. She watched Simoine lead little Isaac to the edge of the group that was wailing their farewells. The little boy raised a chubby arm and waved to Ruthanne. She forced herself to smile and returned his wave.

Tom set his empty coffee mug on the kitchen table and looked over the newspaper at Elizabeth.

"Have you thought anymore about where we're going to take our vacation? I'll need to get my time on the schedule for July soon." He disappeared behind the paper once again.

"Not really," Beth said slowly, pushing a spoon around in the remains of her soggy cereal. "Maybe we don't need to go anywhere this summer, or we could wait until the fall."

The unspoken truth of it all was that Elizabeth was going nowhere until they had heard from Corinne. What if she came home suddenly? What if their cell phones didn't work while they were away and she tried to call them? At least they had a landline at home.

"Not go anywhere? Really, Beth?" Tom folded the newspaper in half and laid it next to his cereal bowl. He looked at his wife in disbelief. "I think we both could use some time away. How about a few days in Toronto or maybe New York City?"

Elizabeth knew he was trying to please her, but a vacation wasn't the answer. She picked up her spoon and bowl, rinsing them before putting them in the dishwasher. Tom stood with his bowl and coffee cup in hand. She took the dishes from him and quickly placed them on the appropriate racks. When she turned to grab the dishrag to wipe down the counter, Tom stood next to her at the sink. She willed herself to meet his gaze.

The Time Under Heaven

"Come on Beth, what's the matter? Talk to me about what's bothering you." His eyes were full of concern, but how could he be so totally oblivious to the real issue? She quickly concentrated on running the rag under the faucet.

"Nothing is wrong. Absolutely nothing. I just don't want to go on vacation this year." She saw the hurt and bewilderment in her husband's eyes. She just wanted him to hold her close and promise he would go find Corinne and bring her home. Tears flooded her eyes unexpectedly. She angrily grabbed a hand towel and wiped them, trying not to let Tom see her lose it. He hated tears and predictably had already left the room.

5

*T*he sand was warm. The tide lapped tentatively at her bare feet, and wet sand squished between her toes. Strident gull voices filled the sky. She shaded her eyes against the dazzling sunlight dancing on the ocean. The water was mesmerizing, even spell-like. Further up the beach, a small girl trotted joyfully toward her with a scallop shell in her hands.

"Ruthanne darlin', can you hear me?"

The scene began to evaporate before her eyes. The voice was barely recognizable and so far away. Ruthanne struggled to hear it again.

"Ruthanne?"

Her lips were dry, and her throat felt like gravel. She forced her eyes open and tried to focus on the face next to her bed.

"Hey there, lady. It's about time y'all woke up. I've been here for ages already." The voice was warm, and there was more than a hint of a Southern drawl. It was a Savannah, Georgia drawl to be exact. Ruthanne finally focused on the face. Nannette Singletree sat in the upholstered chair next to her bed that barely contained her generous size. Short curly white hair framed a cheery, plump face. Her dark brown eyes behind wire-framed glasses showed both concern and happiness at seeing her friend. Nan was the headmistress of Blue River Academy, a boarding school for expatriate and missionary kids. Not only was she a crackerjack educator and administrator, her cooking was legendary. The annual trip to the States meant a suitcase full of grits, pecans, sharp cheddar, and anything else she could haul back.

"Nan!" Ruthanne finally managed to croak. "When did you get here? How did you know?"

"A little birdie told me, since my good friend didn't see fit to," Nan chided in a motherly tone.

Ruthanne sighed and closed her eyes. "No, I didn't," she agreed. "It was so fast, and well, I didn't think..." The complications after her surgery had come just two days before her flight to New York. The mission office had scrambled to change her itinerary. She wasn't even sure they'd allow her fly back now.

"Y'all didn't think for sure. And of course I'd want to be here. It's a good thing Megan Kauffman got a hold of me."

"Megan called you?" Ruthanne struggled to sit up in the bed. Nan helped her adjust the bed and fluffed the pillows behind her.

"Yes. Now, girlfriend, tell me what's goin' on." Nan plunked herself back into the chair, arms folded. She listened impassively to Ruthanne's explanation. The hysterectomy was only the beginning. There were suspicious spots on her liver. The oncologist had already told her to plan on chemotherapy and probably radiation.

"Have you told your sisters what's goin' on?" Nan asked.

Ruthanne reached for the large plastic cup of water and drew a long drink through the straw.

"So you haven't, have you?" Nan pressed.

Ruthanne concentrated on setting the cup carefully onto the tray table over her bed.

"Not yet. My plan is to go back to finish the school. I'll make arrangements after that to go to the States."

She knew her words sounded crazy when Nan's expression turned incredulous, with wide eyes and lips parted. Her friend was momentarily speechless.

"Sugar, you can't be serious. I can't believe your doctor would even recommend such a thing."

Ruthanne looked away, gazing out of the window onto the broad green lawns. The bright colored flower print curtains joyfully framed the view.

"He hasn't, has he?"

Ruthanne ignored the question. "I've fought long and hard for the school. It's going to make a difference in the lives of hundreds of children and their families. It's another way to introduce little ones to the Savior and teach them to read the Scripture for themselves. Plus the school can be used on weekends and evenings for adult Bible studies and other classes. Too much time and effort have gone into the permits. You of all people should know that."

"Whoa! Slow down. I know all the work that's gone into that school. We're cut from the same bolt of cloth when it comes to finishin' a thing."

Ruthanne pulled her legs up, the sheet draped like a tent over her body.

"You think I should go back now? When we're so close?" Ruthanne's weak voice suddenly found strength. She squirmed to sit up taller in the bed.

"I want my friend to be around for a long time," Nan said, turning back to meet Ruthanne's eyes. Nan walked to the bed and took Ruthanne's cool, strong, blue-veined hand. "A very long time. Sometimes we take too much on ourselves or think we're irreplaceable. You've done what you could. It's time to take care of yourself." She paused. "Megan tells me that Stephen has taken over."

A shadow of anger crossed Ruthanne's face. She drew her hand away, considering how to respond. Stephen was giving up seeing his children to continue the school construction. How could she complain? Maybe it was just plain old pride. An inconvenient verse popped into her mind—"God opposes the proud, but gives grace to the humble." Was God opposing her, even though she was doing this all for Him? She desperately needed grace though. A lump in her throat caught her words.

"Yes. Yes he is," she whispered.

A nurse walked briskly into the room with a blood pressure cuff.

"Looks like it's time to skedaddle. I'll be back tomorrow," Nan said. "Take good care of my friend," she said softly to the nurse and closed the door behind her.

6

The sound of car doors slamming punctuated the laughing chatter in the church parking lot. Family groups visited in the warm late June sunshine. Sunday dinners were calling, and the crowd was beginning to scatter. Beth stood talking with two of the newest additions to her women's Sunday School class. They had just started attending Hope Fellowship a few weeks before, and she was anxious to make them feel at home. Both were mothers of teenage daughters, which gave them an instant bond. Beth encouraged them to have their daughters try out the youth group that met on Wednesdays. She glanced over at the brick entrance of the church. Tom and Pastor Howe were deep in conversation. The sermon had been about making the most of opportunities. She wondered what opportunities she'd missed along the way. She'd never finished college. Instead, marriage to Tom had been the most important thing on her mind instead. Maybe the teaching career she'd sought in the beginning would have taken her on a different path. What if she'd dated...she searched for the name, although the face came back to her with amazing clarity. Blond hair, a football player. He'd been a running back or something like that. She forced herself to focus on the conversation that hummed around her.

"Elizabeth, thanks for that great lesson today," Sarah Crider said. "I get so much out of the Bible with the way you explain things."

Nora Tracyzk nodded in agreement. "You do make it so understandable." The two women seemed genuinely appreciative. The warmth of their praise brought a lightheartedness to her that she hadn't felt for awhile.

"I'm glad you think so. Most of the time, I feel like I've made it more confusing," she laughed. She saw Tom shake the pastor's hand and head for their car. "I have to go, ladies. I'm sure my roast is quite done, and it looks like Tom is hungry. Don't forget about youth group for your girls. It's 6:30 on Wednesdays."

Nora and Sarah said their goodbyes. They collected children and husbands, strolling toward the back of the parking lot. Beth caught up with Tom, who was strangely silent. His hands were thrust in his pockets, jingling the bit of change he always carried. His handsome face was marked with worry. She hesitated to ask. It was probably something to do with a church matter. Only last year, the deacons and pastor had asked John Markham, the music director, to resign when he'd been arrested for DUI. He and his wife Joan had finally admitted that he'd had a drinking problem for years. They'd gotten counseling and help for the man and his family. But it had created a terrible strain on Tom and the rest of the men as they tried to keep the damage to the church at a minimum. The new director had started at the first of the year and was doing well with the choir and small orchestra. She hoped it wasn't a church staff matter again.

"Anything wrong, Tom?" she asked as she buckled her seatbelt.

His hands gripped the steering wheel, and she knew he was deciding whether or not he would tell her what was going on.

"I hope it's not another church issue. We need a rest from those."

Her husband was still silent. Only a couple of cars remained in the parking lot now. The tires crunched over the gravel as Tom looked both ways at the exit before pulling out into the now quiet street. He looked over at her, meeting her eyes briefly.

"No. It's not a church issue. Kelley got an email from Corinne." The statement was without emotion. He'd already looked back to the street and made a left hand turn onto Pleasant Ridge.

Beth's heart lurched and dropped like a stone. Kelley was the pastor's daughter. Corinne and Kelley been good friends since junior high and roommates their first year at college.

"Is she all right? Did Corinne say she's coming home?" The words tumbled out. Her heart was beating madly, her hands trembled.

"She's OK. They're in New York City from what Ben said."

"What else? Did she say anything else?" Her mind was in overdrive. Traveling the world had suddenly become a six-hour road trip to New York. Was she living on the streets? Did she have enough to eat? And God forbid, was she using drugs or pregnant?

"I don't know, Beth. Ben didn't have a lot of details from Kelley. Maybe you could give her a call and see if you can find out anything else."

He pulled into their driveway and pushed the button on the garage remote clipped to the visor. The door rolled up slowly, and he drove in. Beth looked down at her clenched hands and willed herself to exhale. She nodded wordlessly, trying to remember if she had a number for Kelley. A call to Kelley's mother Tricia would be first, she decided.

The afternoon had been full of phone calls and checking email before Beth finally sat down. Paul, Sonya and the children had left after the weekly family dinner and naps. Paul had printed off the email Kelley had forwarded. It was short and not detailed, but a sense of relief rinsed off a layer of worry she'd been carrying around for months. Corinne was waitressing while Trevor played guitar as a street musician. They'd found a room to rent that they could afford. They weren't on the streets at least. There was no hint of coming home. There were no questions about her parents. At least she hadn't said to keep the email from them. Beth sighed, leaning back against the back of the sofa and rubbed her temples. A headache threatened like a looming thunderstorm. She looked over at her husband. Tom had been strangely quiet during the afternoon, making hardly any comment on the email or anything else. Now he sat in the recliner, dozing, with the newspaper strewn across his lap. Tears stung her eyes as she watched him sleep. Her anger was like sour curdled milk. Deciding to take a walk, she made certain to slam the door when she left.

Melody wearily dragged her body from the car. She'd worked 14 hours straight, and all she wanted to do was go to bed. Young CNAs were notoriously irresponsible on the weekends about showing up. If she was ever in charge, they wouldn't get a second chance. It didn't matter; the overtime would come in handy to pay the electric and cable bills. They were due again, and the checking account was dangerously low. Looking around at the yard, she suddenly noticed that it was mowed. The lawn mower sat by the side door into the kitchen. "Finally," she said out loud. "It's about time."

Why he couldn't put the mower back in the shed was an unsolved mystery. She'd have to do it. Pulling her small duffle bag and a purse from the backseat, she walked to the front door. At least Dennis wasn't home to demand that she cook him something. His expensive pickup wasn't in the driveway. He was probably watching a baseball game at a buddy's house, or he might be playing softball. She vaguely remembered he'd mentioned something about joining a league for the summer. The house seemed unnaturally quiet as she tossed the bag on the floor and put her purse on the kitchen counter. The TV wasn't blaring, and glancing around the small kitchen, she noticed that the counters were spotless; no beer cans were lying around. No dishes remained in the drying rack; the stove even gleamed.

"It's a day of miracles," she said to the empty room. The small scrap of paper on the kitchen table caught her eye as she grabbed a stale chocolate cookie from the opened package next to it. It simply said, "Mel—had to go. Sorry for everything. –D"

7

Heathrow streamed with people, hurrying to the next gate. Ruthanne watched families struggle to keep children together while managing carry-on luggage. A baby, with a pink sunhat and strapped into a backpack, squalled relentlessly on her mother's back. The woman, whose long black hair was pulled back in a hair band, looked like she was twenty-something and exhausted. Her round, pale face was smudged with travel fatigue. She pulled on the hand of a stubborn toddler, a girl dressed in white sandals and a yellow-flowered short set. The dark-haired defiant child had obviously had enough of travel. She'd decided to sit down in the middle of the foot traffic. The steady rush of humanity, all looking annoyed, pulled their wheeled luggage around the scene. Ruthanne automatically bent to soothe the child. She stopped midway, feeling the healing incision tighten uncomfortably. She straightened gingerly, exhaling slowly. Her eyes met the harried expression of the young woman.

"Traveling is so hard for little ones," Ruthanne crooned. "Come on, sweetheart. Let's see if we can find the big airplane with Mama."

Jerking the child to her feet, the woman said fiercely, "I've got this handled. Jordan, get over it and let's go." The crying child gulped mid-sob and looked back at Ruthanne as the trio plunged back into the crowd.

"We're back in civilization, Sugar," Nan chuckled.

"And you wonder why I don't want to leave Africa," Ruthanne grumbled, adjusting the raffia tote bag on her shoulder.

"I understand only too well. You weren't really goin' to try liftin' that child, were you?"

"No. Of course not," Ruthanne answered. She smiled weakly. It was obvious Nan didn't believe a word of it.

"That's good," Nan said, looking askance at her. She leaned on the handle of her large red leather carry-on. "Now, let's find your gate. You're sure you'll be all right gettin' to New York? I can still change my ticket. Atlanta can wait for a few more days."

Ruthanne shook her head. "I don't want you to change your plans. The mission has someone meeting me at JFK. I'm feeling fine. Really fine," she added in an attempt to sound sincere. She wished mightily for a soft bed and hours of sleep. The doctor had hesitantly given her clearance to travel 2½ weeks after the surgery. She must not lift anything other than her tote bag, which contained her small Bible, passport, wallet, pain medication, and a comb.

The cabin lights were darkened, and the lights on the wing of the plane winked in the twilight. The sky was streaked with sooty grays and shots of mauve. Ruthanne settled into the deep, comfortable first-class seat. She had a feeling that Nan had arranged for this wonderful accommodation for the last leg of the trip. The proper British flight attendant with a soft voice and bright smile brought her a cup of steaming cup of tea and helped her adjust the seat. The roar of engines and the lift into the air brought a wave of uncertainty and anger.

The mission had decided she must return to the States for treatment. Stephen would finish the school project. After her chemotherapy, the board would discuss the disposition of her return. She clutched the Royal Albert china teacup that warmed her hands, ruminating about the total loss of control over her life in the last three weeks. She'd sent a short email to Beth from the hotel in London last night. She'd merely let her sister know that an unexpected trip home was in progress, and she'd call Beth once she arrived in the States. Beyond that, she gave no explanation. There would be a few days of debriefing in New York, and then she'd have to contact her sisters. Then she'd need to stay with Beth. She couldn't impose a cancer patient on the friends in Manhattan.

The call to her family doctor, Dr. Estabrook, had yielded a recommendation for a Dr. Ruiz. She smiled, thinking about their conversation. The sound of his confident, booming voice and the small talk he offered about Sheffield had surprisingly given her a sense of comfort. Dr. Estabrook had made the initial contact and took care of getting her records to the oncologist. Sheffield was only 45 minutes from Rochester. There would be six months of treatment, most likely. Six months before she could even consider returning. The school would be finished by August, and she wouldn't be there to open the doors to the swarm of laughing Maasai children, eager to find a desk of their very own. She wouldn't be the first to write on a pristine blackboard or guide them through the learning games on the new computers. The software had taken months to select and then more months to get the company to donate it.

She closed her eyes and tried to pray. Her mind raced with the list of disappointments. Was this how Job felt when he sat in sackcloth and ashes, scraping his boils? She sighed and took a sip of the cooling tea. That might be somewhat overstated. But it was quite possible she wouldn't ever get back. The chemo or radiation might not work, and the mission might not clear her. It was all out of her hands now. She wished she could let it go. Stephen had tried to comfort her in their last phone call. What had he said? The verse came back from 1 Corinthians 3, "So neither he who plants nor he who waters is anything, but only God, who makes things grow." It didn't matter who did the work or what work. It was God who made things grow. But it did matter—to her. There was so much to do yet. Stephen didn't know the people like she did. They didn't trust him like they trusted her.

The Time Under Heaven

The strain of two days of travel brought a surge of pain and tiredness. She found the brown bottle of pills in her bag and swallowed one with the last gulp of cold tea. Replacing the bottle in the bag, she pulled out her Bible. The thick small square of drawing paper was easy to find in the thin pages. She lovingly looked at the colored pencil drawing of a brown-haired little girl in a blue sundress, picking up a shell on the beach. The drawing never failed to bring joy and pain at the same time. Carefully returning it between the gilt-edged pages, Ruthanne rested her hands over the worn cover and slept as the jet sped through the endless starry sky.

8

"He's left me! High and dry. He took everything out of the checking account," Melody sobbed.

Beth gripped the phone, guiltily delighted to hear that that her ne'er-do-well brother-in-law was gone. Maybe her sister could finally get her life on track. She'd have to talk to her about getting back in church. As the conversation wore on, it appeared that Dennis had taken off a week ago with an old buddy from high school or an old girlfriend. Beth tried vainly to understand the half-hysterical torrent. Dennis had called that morning to tell her he'd scrape enough money together for a divorce. Then the reality of Melody's situation overshadowed the perfect moment of what Beth considered a good thing for her baby sister. It probably meant she'd expect them to pay for everything now. Or even worse, she'd want to live with them. Tom would be livid.

"So, what are you going to do?" Beth asked, afraid of the answer.

"The landlord's given me two weeks to get out. I can't afford the rent on this place. There's a new nurse at work who's looking for a roommate. She's got a two-bedroom apartment at The Willows. I guess I'll see if that'll work out. He emptied the checking account, Beth. I don't have anything! I have just a little cash until next week." The whine in her voice grated Beth's thin patience.

She groaned silently and asked, "How much?"

The check sat in plain view on the dining room table. Beth stood next to it. She watched her sister, dressed in pink scrubs, eye the check.

"Listen to me, Melody," Beth began. She had to stand her ground this time. Tom had been adamant about that. "This is the last check we can give you. Absolutely the last." She was merely echoing her husband's words.

Melody's eyes narrowed. "It will be. I know how Tom feels about me. I thought families were supposed to help each other."

Beth had known it would go down this path. It always did when it was about money.

"We have helped you. It's just that...well, we can't keep doing this." Beth picked up the check and handed it to her sister. The blue eyes were stormy with temper and pain. The once beautiful face looked even older. Impetuously, Beth reached for Melody and hugged her. Melody stiffened her body and pulled away from her sister.

"I've got to go." Melody's voice was terse. "Thanks for this," she finished, holding up the check. The phone rang, startling both women.

"Wait. Wait a second before you go," Beth pleaded. She didn't want another angry departure. Melody shrugged and waited for Beth to answer the phone in the kitchen.

The chatty Lydia at Dr. Estabrook's office greeted her. She couldn't believe what the woman had to say. How could Ruthanne have done this to her?

"Bad news?" Melody asked when she returned to front door.

Beth met her sister's questioning gaze. "I'm not sure. That was Lydia Stowe. You know, she's the receptionist at Dr. Estabrook's. She just asked me if Ruthanne was home yet."

"Ruthanne? I didn't know she was supposed to be home."

"Neither did I. But Lydia said Ruthanne called them a week ago and asked to talk to the doctor."

The deli was filled with a boisterous lunch crowd. The noise was incredible. The high ceiling only helped accentuate the sound. People jostled each other to get in line, many looking at the large menu board behind the counter. A huge jar of dill pickles sat by the cash register, and the smell of roast beef, fresh bread, and sauerkraut filled her nostrils. She'd forgotten the joys of eating in New York. The simple diet of rice, chicken, and vegetables seemed far away as a sensory overload threatened to weaken her knees. It was one of the reasons she dreaded coming back. It was all so overwhelming—choices, noise, people, traffic. Her head ached with tension. Rick and Leah Long managed to press through the humanity and find a corner booth that was just being vacated by four large men in dark suits. While Leah and Ruthanne slid onto the red vinyl bench seats, Rick went to the counter to order.

"I hope this isn't too much for you," Leah yelled, leaning over the gray Formica-topped table to be heard over the din.

Ruthanne smiled, hoping she looked better than she felt.

"I have to get a hot pastrami on rye when I come to the States," she shouted back.

Rick and Leah were part of the mission headquarters staff. Rick was brash and tall, with thinning red hair, combed straight back. Leah, petite and reserved, had a gift for making anyone feel at home. The couple assisted returning missionaries as they transitioned back into Western culture. Their home, a large apartment in Manhattan, had been a quiet oasis for the jaded nerves of many missionaries over the last 20 years. The last two days had been restful and re-energizing. The mission board debriefing had been relatively short, giving her more time to recover from jetlag.

Rick, once a successful stockbroker, had left the pressures of his profession 22 years ago, when he'd met Leah and Jesus all in the same week. He laughingly told the story of spying a beautiful dark-haired woman walking down the street. He followed her to try and initiate a "chance" meeting and wound up in a small storefront church, sitting next to her on a rickety chair as part of a small congregation of 40 or 50. The Second Chance Church's young, passionate pastor preached on the rich, young ruler who'd asked Jesus what he needed to do to inherit eternal life. Rick had taken Jesus at His word, sold his partnership in the brokerage, and hadn't looked back. He and Leah were married six months later in the little church and found positions at the Hope for Africa Mission. Their two sons were now in college; the oldest was preparing for the pastorate.

Rick slid into the booth next to his wife and announced that the food was coming. He plunked a tall metal card holder that gripped a white card with the number "47" in the middle of the table. The crowd began to thin. The volume went down several notches and their conversation resumed at a more normal level. They reviewed Ruthanne's plans to call her family and then take the train to Rochester when arrangements were finalized. It was odd that Elizabeth hadn't responded to her email, but maybe they were away. She'd convinced Rick and Leah that the train would be much easier even if it meant a longer trip. The train ride would give her more time to think. There was no sense in rushing the family reunion. The last time she'd been home, it had been for her mother's funeral, five years ago. Everything had been rushed then.

Poor Mama. The stroke had affected the use of her right side, robbing her ability to write, and more importantly, to draw. Beth had been a trooper, visiting her every day in the nursing home during the few months their mother had lived following the initial stroke. Of course, Mel had done her part as a nurse at the facility.

Forcing herself back to the table conversation, Rick was reviewing train schedules and getting her to Grand Central Station. A pretty waitress with honey-colored hair accented with a swatch of red in the front, walked toward them with plates balanced in her hands and halfway up one arm. The size of the sandwiches was enormous. Ruthanne couldn't imagine how she'd ever eat even half. The doe-like brown eyes and attractive smile caught her attention as the waitress put the plates down in front of them. The face was very familiar.

"Corinne?" she asked in surprise.

9

Elizabeth had been on the phone almost the entire afternoon. Ruthanne was coming home. How could they have missed her email? Of course, true to form, she hadn't tried to call until today to make sure they'd gotten it. The Missions Committee and Tricia Howe, the pastor's wife, now knew she'd arrive by train in Rochester on Thursday. Ruthanne was recovering from some surgery and needed peace and quiet. That must be why she'd contacted Dr. Estabrook. There would have to be at least a small gathering of the committee and the Howes. It was only right since the church provided a major portion of Ruthanne's support. She'd promised Ruthanne it would be low key, which meant that a casual cookout was probably best. She jotted down a quick list for the grocery store. There would be 17 of them. Elizabeth ticked off the faces in her mind. She'd ask for some desserts and a couple of salads to fill out the menu. Then there was the bedroom she needed to get ready. The phone rang, interrupting her progress to the stairs and the linen closet.

"Hey, Beth. It's me," Melody's voice rang out happily. "I just got your voicemail. Wow! This visit's kinda sudden. What's up with Ruthanne? Is she all right? What kind of surgery did she have?"

"I'm not sure. She was vague as always. I just know the mission sent her home to recuperate. She said she'd fill us in once she arrived. Can you come for a cookout on Thursday night?"

"I'm supposed to work 3 to 11, but I'll switch with somebody. There are a couple of people who owe me big time."

Elizabeth hesitated before she plunged ahead to the instructions. The last thing she needed was Melody showing up in a skimpy outfit in front of the Missions Committee and the pastor.

"Uh, Melody. I just want you to know that some folks from church will be here too. It's kind of a welcome-home party. You know."

"Oh." Melody's voice was flat. "I thought it would be just family her first night."

"Ruthanne seemed to want to have everyone all at once. She really needs rest. Our church does give her a substantial amount of support, so the committee needs to talk with her. You understand. Besides we'll have lots of time to spend with her. She's going to be home for six months."

"Sure, whatever. Do you want me to bring anything? I can help with something."

Elizabeth closed her eyes, desperately trying to come up with something without insulting her baby sister. Bringing the hamburger buns or chips wouldn't do.

"I think I have it covered, but if you've got time, could you make Mama's peanut butter cake? It's Ruthanne's favorite."

Melody's tone brightened. "Sure. I think I still have the recipe somewhere. What time on Thursday?"

The train clattered along the tracks, and the lush upstate New York scenery flashed past the window. Ruthanne rested her head against the back of the seat, watching black and white Holsteins graze. A procession of red barns and white houses rose and fell over the rolling green hills. Quite different from the small huts and rangy cattle she was used to, but the old familiarity was calming. It was good to be out of the busyness of the city even though she loved staying with Rick and Leah. Their hospitality was legendary and with good reason. She felt stronger than she'd been in a long while. The comfortable bed, the peacefulness of their home, and their sincere love had eased her back into American life.

But she should be back working on the school. It was possible all the tests were wrong. If the oncologist did new tests, they could prove she was cancer free. God could heal her. He could without a doubt. She'd seen it before. A young Maasai boy named Katawah had been dying. The ugly pus-filled wound on his calf had sent a deadly red streak up the leg. With no doctor at the time or antibiotics available, Ruthanne and a small group of women had prayed and read Scripture with the terrified parents for three days. The boy had slipped into unconsciousness the second night. His exhausted mother had put yet another cool wet rag on his head the third evening, when Ruthanne finished reading the passage about Jairus' daughter. She'd impulsively taken the boy's hand, and his eyes flickered open. She smiled, remembering the look on the mother's face. He'd sat up a few minutes later and drank deeply from the tin cup kept next to the pail of water. All things were possible with God.

Stephen had emailed her that there was a delay in the electrical wiring installation yesterday. A foreman had gotten angry, walking off the worksite, and no one had shown up the next day to complete the wiring. She'd sent a quick reply to tell him who he should talk to. If she'd been there, it wouldn't have happened. Keeping the workers on task and happy was an art, and Stephen didn't have that experience. She absently drew circles with her index finger against the window. Why wasn't she there?

The next few days would be draining. Tom and Beth would meet her at the train station, and she'd need every bit of strength to deal with the onslaught of people. Beth couldn't help herself. Everything had to be an event. At least the brunt of it would be taken care of tonight. She closed her eyes, lulled by the humming and rocking of the train.

The sand was warm under her feet, the tide licking at her ankles. A seagull called overhead, and the sunlight danced off the blue water lapping at the sand. Scents of fish, salt, and seaweed filled her lungs. She ran forward toward the woman who sat sketching on a large white pad, with her knees serving as an easel. The face was hidden by a large brown straw sunhat; colored pencils lay scattered next to her on the glittering amber sand. A dark-haired baby sat on a blanket next to the woman, chubby arms reaching out toward the waves.

The motion of the train slowed and finally lurched to a stop. Ruthanne jerked awake, grabbing the armrests to steady herself. The dream had left her uneasy. She rubbed her temples trying to blot out the feeling.

10

Darkness shrouded the deck sheltered by large maples. A whisper of a breeze broke the stillness of the warm night. The last goodbyes had been said to the church group. The sound of car ignitions and laughter drifted to the backyard where Ruthanne sat staring at the embers of the small, unnecessary fire in the domed, wrought-iron fire pit. Melody had disappeared to the edge of the yard. The glow of a cigarette revealed her location by the snowball bushes. Tom strolled out from the open sliding glass doors off the family room.

"You're off the hook with Beth now. I hope you've survived," he teased.

"Barely," she laughed. "I knew it would happen. That's why I wanted to get it over with tonight." She stretched her long legs out from the wicker chair and yawned.

"You've had quite a day. Where's Melody?" he asked searching through the darkness.

Ruthanne pointed to the red glow at the back of the lawn.

"Ah. Right."

The light disappeared. They could just make out her form coming toward them.

"Everybody gone?" Melody huffed. She wore Bermuda shorts and a tank top.

"Yes. They're gone," Tom answered.

"And none too soon for me. I need to get some sleep." Ruthanne slowly stood, holding her abdomen.

"You do need to rest. My hysterectomy put me out of commission for quite awhile," Melody said, watching her sister closely. "You've lost a lot of weight. That's not all there is to this, is it? Did you get malaria?"

Ruthanne shrugged. "We've got time to talk about it."

Elizabeth appeared in the doorway to the deck. Her face was rosy from her hostess duties. She slipped an arm around Tom's waist. He looked at her questioningly and then smiled, wrapping his arm around her shoulders.

"I suppose we need to have a family meeting before we toddle off to bed," she offered.

"Not tonight, Beth. I'm really all in. I'm longing for that comfortable guest room of yours," Ruthanne said lightly. She was drained of the will or energy to continue any kind of conversation.

"Oh. Well, I guess..." Beth's disappointment was unmistakable in her voice.

"Ruthanne's right," Melody agreed. "She's recovering from a major surgery. We can do lunch tomorrow. I don't have to work until 3:00." She grabbed her purse that was stashed behind a large pot of red geraniums.

"That sounds perfect. How about it, Beth?"

Beth forced a smile. "Of course. I wasn't thinking. We have lots of time."

Ruthanne said her "good nights" and gratefully climbed the staircase to the solitude of the bedroom. She slipped out of her shapeless sundress and into the pink, silky nightgown that Nannette had insisted on buying her in Heathrow. She would never even consider buying such a frivolous piece of clothing. It felt delicious against her skin. A dull pain made her catch her breath as she bent to take off her sandals. It was definitely still there, the shadowy, pulsating disease that was greedy to take her life. It was in for a fight, she decided as she knelt by the bed to pray.

Melody stood by her car, her fingers drumming lightly against the roof. Beth rubbed her forehead, feeling a tension headache coming on as she took in her younger sister's medical opinion.

"You think it is? She's lost some weight, but you know Ruthanne doesn't take care of herself."

"I'm sure it's pretty serious. I've seen that "look" too many times." Melody sighed and stared into the darkness. "We'll find out tomorrow at lunch."

"Maybe. She's always been secretive about things. I just don't understand why she wouldn't let her own family know what's going on with her health."

Melody chuckled loudly. "The family? Oh, my gosh, Beth. We're all screwed up. Why do you think she went to Africa? Daddy could be proud of his missionary daughter, and she didn't have to deal with him anymore."

"That's not why she went," Beth countered. "Besides, Mama and Daddy are gone now. There isn't anything to deal with anymore—if there ever was. Growing up in the parsonage wasn't that awful."

"Think what you want. It was no picnic growing up in that house. I've gotta go. See you tomorrow." Melody slammed the car door and pulled away before Elizabeth could get in another word.

"It wasn't so bad, if you did what you were told," she chastised the empty parking space.

11

D r. Estabrook's office was as busy as she remembered. A Norman Rockwell print of the doctor and little boy waiting for a shot hung on the wall behind the receptionist's desk that was encased behind a low counter and a window partition. Two rambunctious toddlers pounded blocks on the small beat-up side table that held a pile of outdated magazines. The mother of the two, obviously the one who was sick, put a hand on a block as it came down on the tabletop. Her nose was dripping, her eyes red-rimmed.

"Guys! Play with the blocks on the floor," she pleaded. "Sorry," she apologized, looking at Ruthanne and the two other adults, one an elderly man and the other a woman who looked like she was somewhere in her 30s.

"No problem for me," Ruthanne chuckled. "They just have so much energy at that age." She wondered if chubby Isaac was doing all right and if Simoine was still attending childcare classes. The pastor's wife was teaching them until she returned.

"I can only hope they'll take naps today, so I can get one in too. My allergies are killing me." As if on cue, she sneezed and grabbed a tissue from the red diaper bag next to her.

The elderly man raised a white bushy eyebrow at the children and closed his eyes. A medical assistant in Tweety Bird scrubs opened the door next to the receptionist and called for Ruthanne.

She sat on the examining table while Dr. Estabrook put his stethoscope on her back and asked her to take deep breaths. He stepped back and sat on the stool next to the table.

"Lungs sound good. Blood pressure is good. Your incision is healing well. How do you feel?" The gray-haired and deeply tanned doctor asked. He was short, about 5'3", Ruthanne guessed. Wiry and athletic looking, Dr. Estabrook was probably in his late 60s. She'd seen him for a checkup each time she was on furlough. He was the only family practitioner in Sheffield since Dr. Astin, her childhood doctor, had retired ten years ago.

"I'm feeling all right. Just tired," she answered. She wasn't ready to talk about the pain that had come back. It wasn't that bad, and it wasn't all the time.

"That's normal for this situation," he said looking at her with sharp brown eyes. "You do need to gain some weight, Ms. Carroll. The chemo will take a lot out of you, and you could stand some meat on your bones."

She sighed. He sounded just like her grandmother. "I know. That was mentioned before I left Nairobi. I'm doing my best."

"Ah, well. Keep at it. He drew a paper from the clipboard resting on the chair next to his stool. "Here's the address for the oncologist in Rochester. He's a good doctor." He glanced up and smiled. "The clinic is on Richmont, right off 390. Have your blood work done before you see him next week. Here are the orders for that."

She willed herself to take the offered papers. The doctor was saying something else, but her racing mind was thousands of miles across the ocean.

"Any questions?" The doctor's deep voice broke through her daydream.

"No...no. I think you've answered everything."

Elizabeth laid three places at the kitchen table. She looked at her watch. Ruthanne should be back from the doctor anytime. She had to admit that Melody was right. Their sister was very thin, but she'd just had surgery. Good home cooking and lots of rest would certainly fix that in no time. She'd make sure of it.

The front door opened, and Melody called out, "I'm here."

"In the kitchen, Mel," Elizabeth answered.

Melody was dressed in her scrubs; a cheery blue print spattered the shirt, and the pants were navy. Her hair was held back from her face with two small barrettes. She looked almost childlike for a moment, Elizabeth mused as she looked up to see her sister breeze into the kitchen.

"Where's Ruthanne?"

"She should be here any minute. She had a doctor's appointment."

"Oh," Melody said, her index finger tracing around the bottom of a red ceramic bowl of potato salad sitting on the kitchen island. "I hope she's going to tell us what's really going on then."

"I'm sure she will," Elizabeth sniffed. "We're her sisters, for heaven's sake. What would we hide from each other?"

Melody looked up in surprise and laughed. "You're kidding, right?" she finally gasped.

Elizabeth frowned. "I have no secrets."

Melody raised her eyebrows doubtfully, avoided her sister's gaze, and said nothing. At the sound of the front door opening, both women looked through the kitchen doorway to see their sister enter the foyer.

"Is lunch ready?" Ruthanne asked, dropping her bag on the Deacon's bench by the door.

"Almost. How was the doctor's appointment?" Beth handed a tossed salad to Melody from the refrigerator.

"Fine. No surprises. The incision is healing nicely."

"Good. So what's the rest of the story?" Melody quizzed her with a stern nurse look. Melody put the salad down next to the collection of dressing bottles on the round pine farmhouse table.

"Let's all sit down before we get to that," Beth said hastily, pouring water into the glass tumblers by each plate. She assumed her own version of the stern nurse look that let her sisters know that the sit-down instructions were non-negotiable.

"Ruthanne, say the blessing, won't you?" Beth directed as they settled into their chairs.

Ruthanne smiled. "Because I'm the missionary or because I'm the oldest?"

Beth frowned. A slight smirk curved around Melody's mouth. "Maybe both," Melody said playfully. Ruthanne smiled and bowed her head as her sisters did the same.

"Bless, O Lord, this food to strengthen us for your loving service and always keep us mindful of the needs of others. Amen."

Melody looked up with a surprised smile softening her face. "Mama's grace," she said, reaching for the plate of sandwiches in front of her.

Ruthanne's eyes crinkled as she returned a smile and took a chicken salad sandwich. "You remember."

Beth was impatient to get to the real topic. "Of course, we remember. How many times did we say that at the table?" The awkward silence that fell over the table made her embarrassed. She felt angry and wasn't sure why. She quickly picked up the tongs for the tossed salad and piled the greens high on her plate.

Melody bit into her sandwich and looked expectantly at Ruthanne. "So, are you going to tell us?"

Ruthanne sat back in her chair, playing with her fork that was stuck in a mound of potato salad. "I suppose I need to get it over with."

"Yes, you do, Ruthanne," Beth said, still feeling peevish. Ruthanne was maddening in the way she seemed to avoid talking about anything personal. She'd always been aloof and a loner, especially after she went to college.

"Well, the bottom line is that I have cancer."

Beth gasped, her fork clattering against the plate.

"How bad?" Melody asked matter-of-factly.

"It's pretty bad. It started as uterine cancer, but now they've found spots in other places."

Elizabeth felt the blood drain from her face and tears threaten to spill from her eyes. She bit the inside of her bottom lip to keep from crying.

"So when do they start chemotherapy?" Melody asked, taking another bite of her sandwich. "You are having chemotherapy, aren't you?"

"Actually I have an appointment with an oncologist next week, and we'll go from there."

"Wha..wha..what does that mean?" Elizabeth stammered.

"It means she's really sick. Just like I said," Melody snapped.

"Do they say . . ." Elizabeth paused, failing to stem the tears that had begun to roll down her face. "Do they..."Ruthanne leaned forward, her hands resting on the well-scrubbed surface of the antique table.

"It doesn't matter what they say. All that matters is what God says. There are some things I need to do yet. One of them is finishing the school. The project is too important to leave for long. I can't afford to be sick and in the States."

Elizabeth scraped her chair back from the table. Her mind raged with questions. "I don't understand. Does this mean you're not going to have chemotherapy? Or are you going to have it and just leave?" She left the table and pulled a tissue from the box next to the telephone on the counter.

Ruthanne interlaced her fingers and sighed, sitting back against the chair. "I don't know what I mean. Everything is spinning out of control. It has been for a couple of months. The mission isn't going to let me go back unless I get a green light from a doctor anyway." She stood and joined Elizabeth, who offered a tissue to her sister.

Dry-eyed, Melody stared at her two sisters. "You'll have some choices to make. The patients I see in the nursing home usually decide they don't want any more treatments. They're sick of being sick. There are a few that keep at it, but either way, it isn't pretty."

"Melody, you're absolutely cold about this. How can you talk like that?" Elizabeth was mortified. She'd never seen this cool, almost callous side of her younger sister. She was used to the wheedling Mel, trying to get her own way.

"I'm a nurse. I don't have the luxury of crying about sickness and disease. I'm in the middle of it every day."

"This is our sister!"

"I know. And we won't help anything by getting hysterical. Ruthanne needs a clear head, and so do we if we're going to help her."

Melody wiped her fingers on a white paper napkin, wadded it up, and placed it next to her plate. Ruthanne blew her nose before resuming her seat, while Elizabeth wiped her eyes with another tissue. The phone rang, breaking the thick tension. Elizabeth grabbed the receiver before it could ring a second time. She almost immediately held it out to Ruthanne.

"It's someone named Nannette. She sounds Southern."

Ruthanne laughed. "You're right. As Southern as grits and greens." She eagerly took the phone and left the kitchen.

Melody finished her ice tea, while Elizabeth pushed the pile of salad around the plate.

"What's wrong with you, Beth? You're acting like...well, I don't know what."

Elizabeth put the fork down and covered her face in her hands. "I don't know. I'm not sleeping, I guess. Why is this is happening? I can't take one more thing." Her voice was ragged with emotion. Her mind swirled with fear and confusion.

"What are you talking about? One more thing?" Melody demanded, folding her arms across her chest.

"There are just a lot of things happening right now that Tom and I are dealing with."

"What things?" Melody was insistent.

Elizabeth closed her eyes and took a deep breath before looking at her sister. "It's about Corinne. I've been hoping it would be over by now, but it's not."

"I guess you'd better spill all those secrets you don't have," Melody said with palpable sarcasm.

12

Ruthanne lay on her back, staring up at the dark ceiling, comfortable against the soft sheets on the plush top mattress. One thing she did enjoy when on furlough was a good bed. And one more thing—the largest hot fudge sundae DQ could make. Nannette's offer was so tempting, but things were too uncertain. The vision of a comfortable cottage in Wellfleet brought back a lot of childhood memories—good ones...mostly. She quickly tried to focus on the immediate decision. Of course Beth and Melody thought she should do it. And then there was the appointment with the doctor. It hinged on that. But the invitation from Nannette was open for whenever she could get there.

How would she get there? She didn't have a car, and she didn't want to dip into her travel funds for a rental. Her finances were always on the edge. Churches could easily cut back on missionary support when times were tough. Two had dropped her all together in the last year because of budget issues. She couldn't ask Tom and Beth to give up one of their cars. And then there was the conversation she needed to have with Beth and Tom about Corinne. Should she express vague fears and impressions about this boyfriend she hadn't met? She only knew what Corinne had told her. What had really happened from their perspective? Corinne was certainly hurt and felt coming home wasn't an option, but Ruthanne couldn't imagine the door was shut so that she couldn't. It was yet another reason to stay in Africa—no volatile family situations to deal with.

She sat up and turned on the small lamp on the nightstand. Reaching for her Bible, she opened it to read, and the small drawing fluttered to the floor. How would Mama respond to all of this? She slipped from the bed to pick up the picture. Daddy was always predictable. Bear up under the trial. No crying, no complaining, just get on with it. It was all black and white with her father. No hint of gray had entered into decision making for him. The summers at the Cape were the only times in her childhood she'd been free of the parsonage stigma. She wasn't the pastor's daughter at the beach. She was just Ruthanne Carroll, an ordinary girl. As she sat on the edge of the bed, she thumbed over to the Epistle of James, one of her father's favorite books.

Consider it pure joy, my brothers, whenever you face trials of many kinds, because you know that the testing of your faith develops perseverance.

Daddy did love a good trial. They were always great sermon illustrations. She was tired of the trials though. She held the picture in her hand and willed herself to hear the sound of the ocean and feel the sand under her feet.

Slipping it back into her Bible, she knelt by the bed and prayed familiar words, "Lord Jesus, stay with me, for evening has come and the day is now past; be my Shepherd, guard my heart, and awaken hope, that I may know you better at tomorrow's light. Grant me peace and the comfort of your presence. Amen."

Tom and Beth sat on the deck, tall glasses of ice tea on Adirondack side tables next to them as they watched the stars. The warm night blanketed the big backyard with humidity that held promise of a thunderstorm. Clouds to the west were creeping in, extinguishing starlight as they came. The silence had lengthened between them after she'd told him of Ruthanne's illness and the options she was considering. Ice clinked in his glass as he raised it to take a drink.

"I don't blame Ruthanne for considering the no-treatment option," Tom said. "You know what that was like for my mother. The chemo was horrible. It just made her sick and didn't do a thing."

"I know. But everyone is different. Your mother had other health problems too, and she was older," Elizabeth reminded him. "I don't see how she can even consider it. She's much too young not to fight it. I want my sister to get well and to have every chance." She straightened herself in the chair, and leaned forward, her hands clenched.

"I do too," he answered. "She's had a good ministry for such a long time. It must be frustrating her something fierce not to finish the school."

"I think it is. But she doesn't want to talk about it very much. Melody seems to approve of the no-treatment route, which surprises me."

"What does this Nannette have to say about her decision? Did she talk to Ruthanne about it?"

Beth consciously relaxed her posture, attempting to settle into the large chair. "I don't know, but the offer of a house in Wellfleet during high season is quite a gift. This friend has some real connections. She's the principal of a private school in Nairobi. From what I understand, it's exclusive, and there's lots of money. Ruthanne has mentioned her before, but we talk so seldom about anything ...until now." Beth took a sip of ice tea, the glass slippery with condensation that cooled her hand.

"Now, was Nannette going to meet Ruthanne there? I can't imagine her just going by herself, especially if she's so ill." Tom set his empty glass on the table and leaned forward in the chair, rubbing the small of his back, before resting against the wooden chair with a slight groan.

"I guess it's up to Ruthanne. She can take whomever she'd like with her. I'm not sure if Nannette would fly up."

"Once she sees the oncologist, she can make a better decision," Tom concluded.

Elizabeth was silent for moment. "Maybe," she said at last. "Let's hope she makes right decision."

"For her or for you? It's Ruthanne's choice, you know."

Anger bubbled up in Beth like carbonation from a freshly opened soda can, but she managed to hold back the words that were on her tongue. Collecting the tumblers from the table, she pitched the tea and ice cubes that remained into the flowers that edged the deck. Beth silently stalked to the kitchen, feeling her husband's eyes follow her through the doorway.

13

Beth dug into another cardboard box stuffed with more of Mama's personal belongings. She didn't hear Ruthanne come down the stairs as she pulled out another photo album. It was taking much longer than she'd planned to get everything out for Ruthanne to sort through.

"What are you doing?"

Beth about jumped out of her skin. "Ruthanne! Don't sneak up on me like that!" She got up slowly, her knees already aching from kneeling on the floor. She looked at her watch. "Oh, no. I've got to clean this up. The kids will be here in a few minutes." She closed up the box she'd been examining and hefted it onto the table.

"I could help with the kids. I imagine those three are very busy. At least they were the night I got here."

Beth smiled and shook her head. "You don't know the half of it. That's why you have children when you're young. Otherwise you'd never attempt it. They're like a Category 4 hurricane some days, but I don't know what I'd do without them. They've been my lifesaver, since...since Corinne..." Her voice trailed off. It occurred to her that at some point she'd need to tell Ruthanne that Corinne was off on this crazy trip with a boyfriend they didn't even know. It made her cringe just to think about what they were doing. Now that Melody knew, there was no point in keeping it from Ruthanne.

"Since Corinne left?" Ruthanne asked gently.

Beth looked at her in surprise. "You know? How do you know that?" she demanded.

"I've been trying to decide when to tell you this, but I guess now is a good time." She drew in a sharp breath. "I saw Corinne when I was in New York."

"You what?" Beth sat down hard on a dining room chair. "How...how did you..."

"Let's get the rest of this stuff picked up and I'll tell you," Ruthanne answered.

Beth took the news better than Ruthanne thought she might. There weren't many tears, but her sister's face hardened when Ruthanne mentioned Corinne's stubbornness about her father's ultimatum.

"He was too hard on her. He was right, but it was the way he told her. I should've said something, but I just couldn't." Beth's mouth was pressed into a thin line, her lips almost white. "She'll never come home," she whispered.

"You don't know that," Ruthanne soothed. "My friends Leah and Rick will keep an eye on her. The deli where she works is just a couple of blocks from their apartment."

"I'm glad about that, but I'd give anything just to talk to her. She didn't even email us. She emailed the pastor's daughter. You didn't meet Trevor?"

"No, but I think that any rose-colored glasses she's been wearing are coming off."

She'd decided to keep her own counsel on Trevor for the time being. It really wouldn't help Beth to express her opinions.

"I've prayed that she'd see the truth about him. I don't know why it's taking her so long."

Ruthanne chuckled, "That may be a family trait, don't you think?"

Beth's eyes blazed momentarily. She shook her head and sighed; a faint smile spread over her lips. "You're probably right." She twisted her rings nervously.

There were faint multiple knocks on the front door, and then the bell rang.

"Oh dear, they're here, and I haven't gotten you any breakfast yet." Beth hurried to the front door to be greeted by her grandchildren, who ran toward the family room and the toy box.

Ruthanne got acquainted with her grandnieces and nephew, while Beth made a fresh pot of coffee and scrambled eggs. Emma and Clara watched her warily, but Matthew immediately shared his morning adventure of finding a toad on the driveway. By the time Beth called that her breakfast was ready, all three were commandeering meager portions of her lap as she read *The Cat in the Hat*.

Ruthanne found it was hard to believe that her sister was a grandmother, and it had all happened while she was away. When she'd read the emails and seen the pictures, it hadn't quite been real. They were beautiful. Their warm little hands clutched her arms as she finished the book. She could see why Beth enjoyed them so. Clara was already clamoring for another book, and Beth promptly scooped her up, so Ruthanne could eat her breakfast. The group headed for the backyard, and she could hear Beth's laughter float through the open kitchen windows, while they played on the swing set under the big maples. If she were in Kenya, there would be a crowd of children following her to the large shed that served as a makeshift school. Longing for dark-skinned Maasai children swept through her aching heart as she made herself eat the eggs and toast that were growing cold.

While the children napped after lunch, Ruthanne and Beth returned to the dining room and the assortment of boxes. "Let me move some of these to the living room so we can look at them more comfortably," Beth said as she began carting them to the living room.

"What is all this?" Ruthanne quizzed her sister.

"Well, it's all the things we saved when we cleaned out Mama's house. You'd already left for Kenya, but I packed away a bit for you to go through. There are some things you may want to have." Elizabeth's face was still flushed from hauling the boxes off the table and placing them in front of the sofa.

Ruthanne was puzzled why Beth was so suddenly focused on this task. What would she do with knickknacks and old photos—especially now? She pasted on a smile and feigned interest in the boxes. The musty smell of old paper sifted up through a box of photo albums. She pulled them out, carefully setting them on the sofa. Underneath was a thick, square black portfolio, tied securely with a robin's egg blue ribbon. It was one of Mama's drawing books.

"I didn't know there were any of Mama's drawings left. I have the one portrait you gave me at the funeral. I thought the rest had been thrown out or lost."

Beth stopped rummaging through a box of old linens that were embroidered with cross stitch patterns in bright threads and stood up, stretching her back. Her forehead and nose were shiny with perspiration.

"I guess I thought that one was a photo album. Mel and I only found a handful when she died. After Mama had her stroke, she did some strange things before we had to put her in the nursing home. She even burned a pile of drawings. It was terrible. She was so talented." She took a seat next to Ruthanne, watching her untie the silky ribbon.

Inside the crumbly pasteboard covers lay a pile of their mother's colored pencil drawings. They both gasped at the variety of subjects as they carefully began to spread them out on the coffee table. There were some from the beach, several of their father, with sleeves rolled up and a hoe in his hand, and one of him bent over his Bible, deep in study. Many were of flowers, which they recognized from the large gardens behind the parsonage.

"I thought Mama only drew when we were on vacation," Ruthanne finally managed.

"I thought so too, but I guess not. She must have drawn all the time. How did she do it?" Beth pulled out another drawing. "Look at this one," she exclaimed, holding up one of a white clapboard house. Climbing roses and delphiniums overran a low white picket fence with an arbor in the center that led to the front steps. Two women stood on the front porch waving. "This is Grandma Erickson's house, remember?"

Ruthanne stopped breathing when she saw the drawing. It was just like yesterday. She dug her nails into the soft upholstery of the sofa, attempting to keep her voice steady.

"I do," she said softly.

"Why that looks like you," Beth said, examining the picture, "with Grandma."

"I...I don't know if it is or not."

Beth slid the drawing on top of the others and dug through the pile again. "Oh, my. Who is this?" She drew out a picture of a dark-haired toddler in a pink romper, chubby arms, and a bright smile on a cherubic face, a sand shovel in her hand. "Who had such curly hair when they were a toddler? It couldn't be Mel. She was a blonde. I don't remember any cousins that looked like that. Maybe it was Marie, Aunt Ruth's daughter. But they never vacationed with us, did they?"

The Time Under Heaven

Ruthanne felt the blood drain from her face as she took the picture from her sister's hand. The background was the beach with a sandcastle in the foreground. The bright eyes of the little girl mesmerized her. She glanced at the bottom of the paper where she saw the initials AEC scribbled into the corner with the date, 1983. Beth's commentary on the rest of the drawings faded into the roar of the surf that filled her ears.

14

Melody sat in the waiting room of the oncologist, wishing for a cigarette, but she'd managed another two weeks without one. She couldn't mess up now, especially with Ruthanne home. Her oldest sister had always done everything just right. She'd never even had a serious boyfriend which had made their father happy, and she'd become a missionary. There was no way anyone could compete with that. She dragged the toe of her flip flop slowly across the tile floor.

Why this was happening to Ruthanne was a real mystery. She'd dedicated her life to God, done all these good works, gone to church, and now had cancer. Life pretty much stunk, whether you did the right thing or not. Although she did have to admit that things were all right for her for the first time in a long time. With Dennis gone and the divorce underway, she felt like she actually had a life. He'd even sent her a money order for some of the cash he'd taken out of their accounts. That in itself was amazing. She did miss him though. Maybe he'd call her this week.

Her decision to live with Marci was OK so far. They'd divided up the housekeeping, and each cooked for herself. Marci had been through two marriages and had a son who was in the Army. She was a little older than Melody, probably more Beth's age, she guessed.

She sighed and flipped through a decorating magazine. She looked at her watch again. Ruthanne had been back with the doctor for a while, at least 45 minutes. A nurse poked her head through the door and called for Melody. She dropped the magazine on the coffee table and followed her back into the maze of small consulting rooms and then into a larger, bright office with buttery leather furniture. Fuchsia and white orchids decorated the tabletop of a conversation area along with a bubbling stone water fountain. Live, large ficus trees were strategically placed around the room. What she wouldn't give to work in a place like this. No smell of urine or the chaos of yelling patients. It was orderly, peaceful, and beautiful. The doctor was tall and thin, with dark, slick-backed hair. His smile was easy and seemed genuine. He motioned her to take a seat next to Ruthanne on the large sofa, while he settled into a wide-armed chair. The sleeves of his white coat looked a little too short as he held a chart in front of him.

The choices he laid out for Ruthanne were to the point: aggressive treatment that included both radiation and chemo, a more moderate approach of choosing either chemo or radiation, or no treatment at all. There were no guarantees for any of them. She would definitely be sick if she chose the aggressive treatment, probably not as sick with the moderate, and with no treatment, she could expect to get progressively sicker and have more pain. The window was six months. With treatment, the oncologist thought she'd have 18 months to two years. The cancer had definitely metastasized and had found its way into her liver. Melody looked over at her sister, who sat impassively while he explained each option. Her eyes were dull and tired. Melody wondered if she would even last six months without treatment.

"Are you all right?" she asked softly.

"Yes...yes. I'm fine. It's a lot to take in, although I guess none of it is really unexpected."

"Ruthanne, are you sure you're OK?" Melody looked anxiously at her sister's face. It was obvious she was somewhere else.

Ruthanne took a deep breath, and smiled. "I am. I was just remembering happier days. I know you need a decision. What about radiation therapy? I wouldn't be as sick with that, would I?" She looked up expectantly at the doctor, whose placid expression belied his careful eyes.

"No. Most likely not. Fatigue is one of the biggest side effects with that treatment. Of course, each patient is unique. Our bodies fight off disease and respond differently to treatments. I can tell you what generally happens, but there are no..."

"Guarantees. I know," she smiled and then looked over at Melody. "I think the best choice is radiation. It's important to get well enough to go back to Kenya in the least amount of time. If I can at least be there by the time school begins...." Her voice wavered. "It would be enough," Ruthanne finished.

Dinner had been an emotional affair, with Beth leaving the table in tears, Tom following his wife to comfort her. Melody had called it an early night after that. Ruthanne didn't blame her. Beth had always been the most emotional of the three, although Melody ran a close second. But, Ruthanne reasoned, Melody's tears were usually manipulative in some way. She'd been a rock today though. She'd been glad Mel had been with her and not Beth.

Ruthanne went to her room and scattered her mother's drawings over the bedspread. They told the story, up until about 1995, which she found surprising. Had her father known? Had Mama kept it all to herself all those years? Mama hadn't told Beth or Mel. She put the carefully drawn scenes in chronological order, in vertical columns. The small dates in the right hand corner of each one were her guides, although the order was obvious, at least to her. She placed her Bible on her lap, which was open to Ecclesiastes 3.

> *A time to search and a time to give up.*
> *A time to keep and a time to throw away.*
> *A time to tear and a time to mend.*
> *A time to be silent and a time to speak.*
> *A time to love and a time to hate.*
> *A time for war and a time for peace.*

Her time was apparently running short, unless the Lord worked a miracle in her body. It was time to make peace, time to mend, and time to search. Even though she'd run as far as she could, nothing had changed. The wounds remained in her heart, buried but unresolved. Reaching for the telephone by the bed, she dialed Nannette's number.

The trees were dripping from the night's rain on Saturday morning. Ruthanne inhaled the clean washed air as she walked down the street and three blocks over to the church. She needed to give her presentation on Sunday morning, and the pastor had promised to run through the PowerPoint with her to make sure it worked properly. She was still considering if she should talk to him about what she was calling her Ecclesiastes mission. It would involve both of her sisters and Nannette, who was coming in two weeks. By then, she would have had three weeks of radiation therapy, with one week to go. So far, she'd only been fatigued—she was sleeping far more than she ever had in her life. Beth was cooking magnificent meals as if it was her personal responsibility to get Ruthanne well. She'd actually gained five pounds in the last two weeks. Even though she was tired, walking was invigorating. She was still alive. Sucking another lungful of warm summer air, Ruthanne turned the corner toward the church.

Elizabeth slipped the breakfast plates with their film of egg yolk and jam into the dishwasher. Tom was playing golf, and Ruthanne was at the church. With no one around, it was possible to finally make the call. The number had been easy enough to find online. She wiped her wet hands on an embroidered linen hand towel she'd found among her mother's things with Ruthanne. Swallowing hard, she dug around in the junk drawer to find the yellow sticky note, buried under coupons, business cards, and paperclips. Her hand was shaking as she punched in the phone number. After three rings, a harried voice greeted her.

"Sol's Deli. What can I getcha?"

"Uh, hello. I'd like to speak to Corinne Hartman, please."

"What? Corinne?"

Elizabeth could hear the clatter of plates and people yelling in the background. It was a mistake to call. Why had she done it?

"Yes, Corinne. I need to get a message to her," she plunged ahead, a sick feeling in her stomach.

"She's not workin' today. What's the message?"

Elizabeth exhaled, relieved. "No message, I guess. I'll call another time."

The phone slammed down in her ear, and she pressed the "Off" button on the phone, putting it back in its cradle. Maybe it would be better to send a message through Ruthanne's friends. Their number was around somewhere; she'd seen it in Ruthanne's address book.

The dress rehearsal of her presentation had gone perfectly, which didn't mean anything. It was Ruthanne's experience that computers and A/V equipment were exceedingly temperamental and refused to work at the right time out of spite for human beings. Her notes were placed neatly on the pulpit for the morning.

She looked out over the empty pews, remembering Sunday mornings from years ago in one of the little churches her father had pastored. Mrs. Bernard had pounded the keyboard with a galloping version of "Victory in Jesus," her magnificent girth spread across the piano bench with large arms flapping in rhythm. She smiled at the memory. Her mother was usually with the babies in the small nursery, while the three sisters sat with backs straight and eyes forward on the front row. If one of them fidgeted or didn't have their Bible open during the sermon, their father knew and shot what they called his "laser ray-look" from the pulpit to the offender. There was no technology back then, but her father's fervent sermons were delivered with passion. He would never have allowed slides to dictate the direction of his sermon anyway. Sighing, she stepped from the platform and walked to the large welcome area at the rear of the church with its deep carpet in shades of brown. Pastor Howe and his wife Tricia stood waiting for her. Ben Howe was a little paunchy with salt and pepper hair. Tricia had shoulder length brown hair and a brilliant smile. The couple had been supportive through her treatments. They had taken her to several appointments and checked on her after each one.

"All set, Ruthanne?" the pastor asked brightly.

"I believe so. Thanks for opening up the church today."

"It's no problem. We're here every Saturday," Tricia laughed. "There's always something that we need to do before Sunday."

Ruthanne chuckled. "I know what you mean. Beth and I had to make sure the hymnals and Bibles were straight in the racks every Saturday, while Melody put the bulletins out on the table in the vestibule for the ushers and made sure the crayons were distributed for Sunday School.

"Sounds familiar," Ben Howe smiled, nodding his head. "Are you sure you're up to doing this? You have a lot on your plate right now. We'd certainly understand..."

"I'm sure. It helps me keep my mind off other things. And it's a way for me to share the passion I have for the Maasai."

"You must miss being there," Tricia empathized. "Have you heard any news about the school?"

"I am homesick. I really miss the young mothers and their babies. I got an email from the director this week, and everything is on schedule. They're just waiting for desks, computers, and a backup generator. The school should open by the end of August."

It was a hard pill to swallow. Stephen was doing an outstanding job to complete the school project. He had kept his word, and according to both him and the mission office, the school would open on time. She wasn't as necessary to the project as she'd feared or had she merely hoped?

"Let us give you a ride home. You must be tired from that walk," Tricia offered. She brushed back a strand of brown hair from her eyes.

Ruthanne hesitated for a moment and then agreed. She was tired, and the walk back to Beth's would probably not be as energizing as the walk to the church. The pervasive fatigue gave her second thoughts about broaching her Ecclesiastes mission. She had no energy to discuss it. Thanking the Howes for the ride, she slid from the back seat and walked slowly to the house. Beth was nowhere around, but a note on the counter told her that lunch was ready for her in the refrigerator. A large manila envelope lay next to the note. It was from Nannette.

15

Ruthanne dumped the contents of the envelope on her bed. A sudden breeze from the open window ruffled the papers, revealing photographs and legal-looking documents. She put a hand on the pile and placed her Bible from the nightstand on top, while she closed the window. A thunderstorm was brewing in the west. Dark clouds piled up like pillowy mountains. A growl of distant thunder confirmed what was coming.

The pictures of the house were beautiful. There were four bedrooms, a huge kitchen, with what looked like new appliances. She pulled out the last photo, which was of the exterior. She gasped in recognition. The wraparound porch on the Cape Cod house was framed within a white picket fence and climbing roses. How could this be? The siding on the house was now stained a sandy brown with crisp white trim. She put the photo down and rubbed her forehead in disbelief.

"Oh, Lord it doesn't get any clearer than this. How can I do this? I don't have the strength," she breathed.

Nannette's letter was straight to the point.

My dear Ruthanne,

I know you'll be pleased when you see the pictures of the Brayden House. I had no idea when it was offered to me that it was your grandmother's home. I do believe the good Lord is telling you to go through with this adventure. It needs to be done, and I'll be with you every step of the way. Tell your sisters to pack because we're all going to Wellfleet.

The enclosed paperwork will help us get started. Sorry there wasn't more information, but once we get there, I'm sure we'll have more success. The Lord is on our side.

Y'all take care of yourself until I get there.

Your Lovin' Savannah Sister,

Nan

Ruthanne set the photos aside and blinked back tears as she tried to look at the papers that were out of focus. Grabbing her reading glasses, she examined what Nan had managed to find. There were copies of six birth certificates for girls born on May 24, 1981. There were two more certificates for boys born on the same day. The place of birth for all of them was Hyannis, Massachusetts. None of the parents' names were familiar. This couldn't be it. There had to be more. She looked through the sheets of birth announcements printed from online newspaper archives for dates starting May 23 through May 25, 1981.

Thunder cracked like a shotgun blast, and a stormy wind rattled the window. The branches of the maple outside scratched against the house. Ruthanne jumped;

perspiration trickled from her neck. It ran down her spine, causing her to shiver. She licked her lips and took a deep breath, steadying her nerves. The rain began to hit the window in heavy staccato drops. She stood and watched the rain sluice down the glass. A dagger of lightning splintered the dark sky, and thunder crashed again. She hugged herself, struggling to formulate words that would explain this trip and her dilemma.

"Ruthanne! I didn't think you were home," Beth said behind her. Her hair was flattened against her head; water dripped down her forehead and cheeks. Her shirt and capris clung to her body.

Ruthanne whirled around in surprise, forcing a smile.

"You scared me. What a storm! And I guess you got caught in it."

"You can tell?" Beth laughed grimly. "I'm soaked to the skin. I didn't think you were back yet. Your lunch is still in the refrigerator." Her voice took on a scolding tone.

"You caught me. I was just going down now."

"Did you get the package from your friend, Nannette? I left it on the counter for you.

"Yes. I got it. Thanks."

"Was it information about that house? I know she wants you to go. I'm not sure if you're really strong enough to do a trip like that though." Her eyes were filled with concern.

"Well, that's something I need to talk with you and Melody about," Ruthanne said slowly. "There are some things I need to tell you, and it will involve a trip to the Cape."

"Nannette is perfectly welcome to stay here. You two can have some time to yourselves and do some little trips if you need to get away. You'll be in your own bed every night—"

Ruthanne held up her hand, stopping Beth before she could continue.

"I need to go, and I want you and Melody to go with me."

Beth's eyes widened in surprise. "What do you mean, you want us to go too? What's this about?" Her irritation was obvious.

"I'm sorry to do this, but I have some unfinished business there." She hesitated and then sat down on the bed. "I just know that it's time to finish it if I can. I hope you and Melody can bear with me." She looked at Beth's anxious face and then at the floor, wriggling her toes nervously in her sandals.

Beth sighed, "I'm sure we both want to help you." She twisted the bottom of her wet camp shirt away from her body. "I've got to change. We'll talk while you eat lunch."

Ruthanne smiled bleakly. "Right. I'll call Melody too."

Watching Beth hurry down the hallway to change, Ruthanne felt her stomach rumble with hunger. She'd started everything off wrong with Beth, but her sister was right about eating. She needed to eat. She'd need every bit of strength she could muster in the next few weeks.

"This Nan is renting Grandma's house?" Melody's voice rose in surprise. The three sisters sat around the kitchen table, looking at the pictures Ruthanne had spread out.

"That's right. It's one of the confirmations to me that I need to...well, go back there."

"They've really changed the inside," Beth grumbled. "Grandma's kitchen isn't..."

"It's a gourmet kitchen," Melody shot back. "It looks gorgeous. All of her stuff was so old when we were kids. Of course they've remodeled. The house was sold in '96, right after Grandma died. It was getting really run down."

"I know, but it's still Grandma's house," Beth objected. "It's not the same."

"It isn't, but we have many fond memories there."

"And some not so fond," Melody reminded her. "Remember when Daddy told Grandma she was leading us into sin when she taught us to play Gin Rummy? What a huge fight—the evils of face cards and TV thrown in for good measure." Melody giggled. "Grandma got him though. Don't you remember?"

Ruthanne sat back in her chair, trying to recall the tense scene that had spoiled the last few days of their vacation. It was so long ago. She'd tried to wipe out those scenes that still made her stomach lurch with dread at making her father angry.

Beth looked at Melody quizzically. "What did she do? I don't remember her getting back at Daddy."

Melody smoothed her bangs from her eyes and smiled. "She offered his help to the neighbor whose septic tank had backed up. He couldn't refuse to help a family with four kids. The father had broken an arm and couldn't take care of it. Daddy spent two days next door digging it up and taking roots out of a pipe or something. It was messy."

"Daddy would have helped the neighbor whether Grandma said anything or not," Beth argued. "He was just trying to protect us. You know how he was."

Before Melody could counter, Ruthanne forged ahead. It was the time to speak up. It was the first step of this journey.

"Before we get sidetracked, I need to tell you why this trip is so important to me," she began, her voice steadier and firmer than she'd imagined it would be.

16

Childhood memories were revived as Ruthanne began talking about the annual vacation to Wellfleet. Beth and Mel nodded and smiled as she reminisced about the rental cottage that was reserved every year for them by their maternal grandmother, Marilyn Erickson. An outspoken woman, Grandma Erickson declared it was the only way she would see her grandchildren. Grandma's opinion of her son-in-law, the Rev. Joseph Carroll wasn't glowing. Rather than have him retell an annual tale of woe about his lack of funds for a family vacation, she made sure the Carroll family had the cottage every August. With the enticing offer of free accommodations, their beat-up station wagon made the ten-hour trip. As for their father, he tolerated his mother-in-law, whose ideas of childrearing and just about everything else were in conflict with his, but over the years the tension between the two eased.

"Remember our last vacation all together? I had just finished my junior year of college," Ruthanne continued.

"Sure. It was really rainy that summer. We were stuck inside most of the time with Daddy," Melody shuddered. "He was like a caged lion. It wasn't much fun."

"There were problems in the church that year. He had a lot on his mind," Beth hedged.

"Right. It was a stressful vacation. I spent a lot of time at the library just to get away," Ruthanne strained to keep them on track.

"You were always the student." Melody teased, rolling her eyes.

"Please, I just need to get this out," she pleaded.

Beth gave Melody a reproving look. Melody shifted her eyes to the table, a pout spreading across her face. "I was just kidding."

Ruthanne closed her eyes, still debating with herself. It could be a giant mistake to tell them. She and Nan could do this alone. But the consistent prompting she felt to include her sisters, these women she barely knew anymore, was still there. What would they think of her? All the old fears rushed in; she felt heat seep into her cheeks, and then she started again.

She had met Danny that last summer vacation in the small village library. He'd just finished hiking the New England section of the Appalachian Trail. He'd hitchhiked to the Cape to write about his experiences for a magazine and enjoy the beaches. He was 25 and was attending a seminary somewhere in Pennsylvania. He was experiencing a crisis of faith, after a friend had committed suicide and he wondered if he was cut out for the pastorate. Danny was athletically built and tall. Taller than their father, he had shaggy dark blond hair, an aquiline nose, and piercing gray eyes. They read Robert Frost, Emily Dickinson, and Walt Whitman in the library's small sitting area. They took long walks on the beach in the rain. Somewhere in the midst of helping Danny rediscover his faith, it all went wrong. By the end of September in her senior year at Mt. Grace Bible College, her fears were reality.

Beth sucked in her breath, while Melody stared with saucer-like eyes at her oldest sister.

"You were pregnant?" she asked.

Ruthanne nodded. She clasped the water glass in front of her and took a long drink. Her throat felt like it was full of dust.

"Did you have an abortion?" Beth blurted out. "You came home for Christmas that year. You didn't look pregnant."

"No. I didn't have an abortion. I hid my 'condition' pretty well. I just wore looser tops for a long time. There wasn't a problem until I was about seven months. I couldn't lose my scholarship, and I wanted desperately to finish my degree. How would I have explained everything to...?"

"To our very understanding father," Melody finished bitterly.

"It could have ruined his ministry," Ruthanne asserted. "I couldn't do that to him."

"You told Mama though, didn't you?" Beth asked, rising from the table. She began making coffee as if she needed a task to distract her. A thin stream of dark liquid hissed into the bottom of the carafe. Beth stood staring at the coffeemaker before turning back to her sisters. "She made that trip to your college because you were sick or supposed to be sick."

"I had to tell Mama. I needed her help."

It hadn't been easy for her mother. Ruthanne knew she'd stretched the truth to the limit and beyond. Once she arrived at Mt. Grace, a doctor's note with a diagnosis of exhaustion was obtained. Complete rest was prescribed for eight weeks, which saved the scholarship. No one questioned her temporary withdrawal from school.

Within two days, Ruthanne was whisked away to her grandmother's house on Cape Cod. Annaliese Carroll and Marilyn Erickson made arrangements with a local attorney to finalize adoption papers as soon as the baby was born. Ruthanne had been assured by the two women she trusted the most that the baby would go to a good family. After a tearful and hurried departure by her mother, Ruthanne found refuge with her grandmother.

Six weeks later, Marilyn was present at the birth of her great granddaughter. Ruthanne glimpsed the squirming and squalling tiny baby girl with a mass of wet, dark hair. Nurses wrapped the baby in blue and white receiving blankets, and then she was gone. Ruthanne signed all the papers required by the attorney.

Three weeks later, she returned to Mt. Grace and finished her degree over the summer semester. She was supposed to act as if nothing had ever happened. It was in the past. She'd been fairly successful for many years. Going to Kenya had made it easier to believe it was all a bad dream of some sort. But everything was different now.

"I want to find my daughter. And I'd like both of you to make this trip to the Cape with Nan and me. Look at it as a family vacation. As a bonus we get to stay in Grandma's house." She smiled, blinking back a stray tear that threatened to dampen her cheek.

"I can understand you wanting to find your daughter, but I can't see how we'd be any help." Beth's voice was skeptical.

"I think it's a great idea," Melody plunged in. "A vacation at Grandma's—who would have thought we'd get the chance again?"

"It's definitely a God thing," Ruthanne agreed. "Nan had no idea about the history of this house until I told her about...well, what I just told you. She mentioned the address, and it all clicked." She looked over at Beth, who rubbed an index finger absently across a paper napkin, not meeting her sister's gaze.

"I'll have to ask for the time off. When are we leaving?" Melody's eyes sparkled with childlike anticipation.

17

"Your news didn't seem to faze Mel at all," Elizabeth commented as she cleared the table of coffee mugs.

"No. I guess it didn't, but it did faze you."

Elizabeth stopped putting silverware into the dishwasher and stood up, her hand on the counter. Her expression was a jumble of hurt and uncertainty.

"It did. I'm still trying to digest it all. I can't believe Mama never said a word or even hinted at it. Not ever. I remember her leaving for Mt. Grace to find out what was going on with you. She told us you had been studying too hard and were on the verge of physical collapse. You needed the quiet of Grandma's house to recover. It was all a lie." The tone was bitter.

She rinsed the cups and put them in the top rack. Snapping the dishwasher door shut, she wiped wet hands on a kitchen towel.

"It wasn't all lies. I *was* exhausted from hiding everything from professors and friends. My roommate knew something was wrong, but we never spoke about it. I kept my head buried in the books." She paused, searching her sister's eyes. "Beth, I do want you to come with me. I'd like one more family vacation, and I need your support to find my daughter."

Ruthanne put an arm around her sister's shoulder. Beth visibly relaxed and nodded.

"I'll talk to Tom tonight. It won't be a problem."

It was too late to run when Dennis appeared from nowhere and opened her car door in the apartment complex's parking lot. He leaned up against the fender of a pickup parked next to her. His jeans were creased with dirt, his gray T-shirt stained. He scuffed the pavement with his work boot, as if waiting for her reaction.

"Dennis! What are you doing here?"

"Just wanted to see my beautiful wife. Anything wrong with that?" A leering grin spread across his unshaven face. The smell of liquor hit her nostrils with sickening force.

"You're drunk," she said angrily, slamming the car door and stepping away from him. She put the strap of her purse over her shoulder.

"I've had a couple. No big deal. Hey, let's go out tonight and get something to eat."

"We're getting a divorce. I'm not going anywhere with you."

She turned her back on him and strode toward the doors of the building. His meaty hand grabbed her shoulder and spun her small frame around. Pain shot through her shoulder, and Melody gasped. Shaking loose from his grip, Melody twisted away, trying to run. Dennis grabbed her arm before she took two steps. The look in his eyes sent fear streaming through her body. He bent over her, eyes narrowed, a finger wagging in her face.

"You've got a boyfriend, don't cha? You've had him all along."

"No. I don't have a boyfriend." Her heart pounded like a summer downpour in her ears. She'd never seen Dennis like this. Melody wanted to scream, but she couldn't take a deep breath.

"That's not what Roy says. He saw you the other night with a guy."

She pulled against his grasp, trying to free her arm. "What guy? I haven't been out with anybody."

"Roy saw you in the nursing home parking lot, kissing some guy." Dennis' shaggy hair fell in his eyes, and he swept it back. He teetered forward, loosening his hold on her arm. Melody stepped back, wanting to run, but her body seemed frozen.

"Roy's a liar. It didn't happen. You need to leave, or I'll call…"

She took another step back as Dennis lunged at her, catching the strap of her purse. He glared angrily down at her, twisting the strap to pull her toward him.

"Or you'll call the cops," he taunted. "You'll be sorry if you do. You're still my wife. If I catch you…"

A car swung into the parking lot, catching Dennis' attention. He released the strap and hissed, "Remember what I said."

Half sobbing, Melody ran to the double glass doors into the common area. It wasn't until she was safely in the apartment with the deadbolt thrown that her pounding heart slowed. How could she have missed him—ever? Fumbling for the cell phone at the bottom of her bag, she punched in the number of her attorney. Dennis wasn't going to ruin either her new life or the coming vacation.

Ruthanne sat on the bed with Elizabeth, looking through the drawings that were arranged on the bedspread.

"This is when Mama left me at Grandma's." Ruthanne gently fingered the drawing. "At least she didn't draw me as I really was." She smiled weakly, handing it to her sister.

Elizabeth laid it next to the one of a young teenage girl with long dark hair pulled back from her finely featured face. The deep set eyes were gray; her mouth had a bit of a pout. A sandcastle and beach chairs were in the background.

"This is the last drawing from '95. She would have been 14 years old." Ruthanne went on.

"Mama must have known the family who adopted her," Beth mused.

"She must have known much more than she ever told me. I don't think she even told Grandma much of anything." Ruthanne sat down on the bed and propped a pillow behind her back.

"Most likely it was a family who lived on the Cape. These drawings are all at the beach. Daddy and Mama never went anywhere else on vacation that I know of."

"No. It was always at the Cape. I think she looks like you. She's tall and has that skinny Carroll build."

Ruthanne smiled wistfully. "I guess she does. I see her father in her though. Her eyes are his."

"What about the father? Does he even know? Do you know what happened to him? "

The questions were like machine gun fire. Ruthanne picked up another picture, considering her answer. "He wasn't interested."

Elizabeth raised an eyebrow, but seemed satisfied. Ruthanne didn't want to explore the topic of her daughter's father. That was pain best left buried. He'd been a coward, accusing her of seducing him and implying she'd probably done it many times before. Danny, for all of his charm and apparent sincerity, had only wanted one thing from her.

"How are you going to find her after all this time?" Elizabeth asked, absently glancing at the drawings again. "Aren't adoption records sealed?"

"They are, but I'm hoping someone will remember her, or maybe there's a record of a christening or baptism at one of the churches."

"But you don't know her name or anything, right?"

"Right. But I have dates and these pictures. Someone is bound to recognize her. Wellfleet isn't a big place."

"True. The pictures will help. What if she doesn't live there anymore?"

Ruthanne shrugged. "I haven't thought that out. I'm not sure yet."

Elizabeth carefully stacked the drawings and slid them into a slim brown portfolio. She gave it back to her sister. "What if she doesn't want to, well...meet you?"

Ruthanne grasped the portfolio in her hands and fiddled with the attached ribbon ties. Leaving it on the bed, she stood and walked slowly to the window that looked out over the backyard. Her fingers intertwined behind her back.

"I don't know. The Lord will have to work out the details. All I know is that I need to make this trip. The outcome is up to Him." After the words tumbled out, relief poured through her veins like the first rains of summer soaking into the parched African ground. "I think this all has happened just to teach me that one thing. Trust and obey, just like the song we sang in Sunday School. It's what it all boils down to. I've tried to make it more complicated."

She noticed Beth wince at the statement. After seeing the friction between Beth and Tom, she wondered where their marriage was headed. Melody was making changes, which were probably for the best, but it wasn't the eldest sister's place to give advice on relationships right now. The doorbell rang, allowing Beth an easy exit. Ruthanne curled up on the bed. Weariness had overtaken her body; her legs felt leaden. Sinking her head onto the pillow, sleep came in seconds.

18

The test results lay on the doctor's desk in front of him, while Ruthanne and Nan watched him scan through the contents. Ruthanne noticed the light tapping of Nan's foot on the carpet, and then she realized her own foot was tapping in the same rhythm. Consciously relaxing, she stretched her long legs and folded her hands in her lap.

"It looks good. Quite good, in fact," Dr. Ruiz finally said, looking up from the paper. "Your blood work isn't perfect, but not bad considering. And almost all of the spots on the liver are gone. After you come back from your vacation, we'll talk again. I'd like to talk about another treatment that may get you back to Kenya."

"It's a good report?" Ruthanne was slightly incredulous that he wasn't telling her more bad news.

"A good report, Ms. Carroll. Surprising, but not unheard of." He took his reading glasses off and laid them across the blue manila folder with her name on the tab. "Do you have any questions?"

"As long as she's clear to do this little bit of travelin', doctor," Nan interjected. The worry lines had eased on her forehead, and her dark brown eyes were twinkling. "Sugar, I told y'all that it would be a good report today."

"You think I could get back to Kenya?" Had she heard the doctor correctly? A lump came to her throat just thinking about it.

"Possibly, Ms. Carroll. No promises. But we'll discuss that when you get back. I think this little vacation to Cape Cod is just the ticket after four weeks of radiation therapy. Have some fun, relax, and then we'll talk."

The ride back from Rochester to Sheffield seemed to take forever. Traffic was backed up on the 390 because of an accident, and by the time they exited, both women were frazzled. When they finally pulled into the driveway, cars lined the street. Ruthanne groaned.

"Beth's invited everyone. I knew I shouldn't have called her."

"Sugar, you need to celebrate, and so does your family."

"I'm not cured, Nan. I'm better, but I'm not cancer-free."

"We're celebrating that you're better. Now smile, Honey Bun, and get your grits together."

Ruthanne gave her friend a crooked smirk as she opened the car door.

The church family along with Paul, Sonya, and the kids had gathered in the backyard. That Elizabeth had managed to pull this party together in the space of two hours was astounding. Tom and Pastor Howe were cooking hamburgers and hotdogs over two grills like madmen with spatulas. Their sweaty faces were shrouded in clouds of smoke rising from the unrelenting heat of the grills. The backyard was permeated with the wonderful aroma of burgers. Tom gave a cheer as Nan and Ruthanne appeared on the deck, wiping his forehead on a towel that was tucked into the band of his Bermudas.

The crowd broke into applause, and a male voice began singing "How Great Thou Art." Everyone immediately joined in, voices soaring in grand praise. It took Ruthanne's breath away. Her knees felt weak as tears ran down her face. Nan offered a reassuring hug while Beth guided her to a picnic table on the lawn. The twins and Matthew brought handfuls of daisies and sweet peas from their grandmother's garden. Shyly, they laid them on Ruthanne's lap. Matthew stood solemnly next to her, patting her arm. She bent and kissed his forehead, which he immediately wiped off with his hand. The girls ran back to their parents, who quickly came to offer congratulations. Ruthanne accepted the well wishes of the long line of church family. It occurred to her as she finished a small bit of cake and ice cream in the twilight that Melody hadn't made an appearance, but then again she'd probably had to work.

Elizabeth watched the crowd trickle away to their cars through the kitchen window. Tricia Howe's and Elizabeth's Sunday School class was clearing up the last of the potluck feast that predictably appeared whenever a church party was announced.

"What a night! I hope we didn't tire Ruthanne too much," Tricia exclaimed while she dumped the remains of half-eaten burgers and baked beans into the wastebasket.

"I think she really enjoyed the party, but we'll make sure she sleeps in tomorrow. We leave on Saturday, so I want her really rested for the trip." Beth replied. "Now this will be a celebration vacation rather than what we thought it would be." She took the sprayer from its place on the sink and rinsed bits of garbage down the growling disposal. "I don't know what happened to Mel though. I can't believe she didn't come."

"She may have had to go in to work," Tricia offered.

"Melody could have called at least," Elizabeth groused. "It's typical. Sad to say about my own sister."

Tricia made no reply and folded her dish towel, placing it on the counter.

"Beth," one of the young women called from the foyer. "Please come quick."

Elizabeth, startled by the urgency in the woman's voice, hurried toward the front door. Julie Pratt, one of the young women in her Sunday School class, was ashen, her eyes large with fright. Elizabeth choked back a scream at the sight of Melody, whose face and right eye were swollen and bruised. She rested her right arm limply across the left. Julie caught Melody as she slipped to the floor.

Tom and Elizabeth sat in the ER waiting room with Ben and Tricia while Melody was behind a curtain being examined. It was almost certain that her wrist was broken. Elizabeth hoped her nose wasn't broken too. What had gotten into Dennis? He'd never been violent that she knew of. At least Mel hadn't ever said anything about it. Had she ever noticed bruising or mysterious injuries to her sister before? She couldn't remember ever seeing any. She covered her face with her hands. Tom rubbed her back, trying to soothe her jangled nerves. Tricia got up and offered to get coffee for everyone. Ben left with his wife to help.

"Good. There's the police," Tom commented, looking toward the ER entrance. "I hope she doesn't get cold feet about reporting Dennis. He could have killed her."

Elizabeth watched the policeman talk with the nurse at the circular desk in front of the examination rooms. The nurse, her long brown hair pulled back in a low ponytail, pointed to the area designated with a yellow "3" on the wall.

"I know," she half-whispered. "I hope she's going to be all right."

She got up and paced around the small room, watching the ER activity through the bank of windows as EMTs brought an elderly man in on a gurney. The beeping machines, scurrying nurses, and the smell of hospital made her stomach churn. When would the roller coaster ever stop for Melody? Just when it looked like she might actually get her life together, this happened. It was always something with Melody. She rubbed the back of her neck and then leaned against the coolness of the wall.

Dennis had always been the wrong choice for Mel. It had been obvious from the start that he was all talk. He had no education, no ambition. He'd had good looks and a smooth line, which Mel had fallen for hook, line, and sinker. What a mess! And now what about their Cape Cod vacation? Maybe Mel wouldn't be able to go, which might make everything easier. But Ruthanne had her heart set on all of them going. She must see what stress that would cause now.

She sighed and sat down again. Ben and Tricia appeared from the hallway, loaded with four coffees in a cardboard carrier and single cookies wrapped in cellophane packaging. Her pastor put the coffees on the table, while Tricia unwrapped a cookie and took a bite. Tom reached for a black coffee, blowing on the steamy liquid before taking a sip.

"Any word yet?" Tricia asked, looking toward the windows.

"Not yet," Tom clipped. "It always takes way too long. It reminds me of when we brought Corinne in for that sprained knee she got in summer soccer."

Elizabeth nodded, immediately wondering what her daughter was doing tonight. Was she safe? Did she want to talk to her mother? Would she ever want to come home?

"Mrs. Hartman?" A heavyset nurse in green scrubs stepped through the waiting room door.

"Right here," Elizabeth said, rising from the vinyl upholstered chair.

"Your sister wants to see you now."

Elizabeth followed her behind the curtain, steeling herself for how her sister looked. Melody sat on the exam table, her right eye swollen almost shut. Her hair was matted to her head, and a small butterfly bandage closed a small cut under her left eye. A cast encased her right arm from wrist to elbow. Elizabeth bit the inside of her cheek to keep from crying.

"I know I look pretty bad, Beth. Don't worry, I'll be OK. But I won't be working for awhile. He broke my arm. The doctor says six weeks," She shook her head. "I hope they find him tonight. He's lost his mind."

"Why would Dennis do this to you? Has he been abusive before?"

"No. Never. Unless you count his laziness as abuse."

"Then why?"

Melody sighed and looked at the floor. "He was drunk, and he thinks I'm dating somebody."

Elizabeth frowned. "Are you?"

"No. I'm not dating anyone. One of his friends thought he saw me with a guy. It's not true. This friend's never liked me, and the feeling is mutual. Especially after tonight." She gritted her teeth, sliding toward the edge of the examination table. "I guess I'm ready to go. I've got to get a prescription filled for pain on the way home."

"Let me help you down." She helped Melody maneuver from the table to the floor, watching her carefully. She didn't want Melody passing out again.

It was almost midnight by the time Tom drove into the garage. Melody had insisted on going back to the apartment since her roommate was there. Would the roller coaster with Mel ever end? Elizabeth breathed another prayer for the police to catch Dennis. She saw that Ruthanne's light was still on as she padded past the bedroom door. Knocking softly before turning the knob, Ruthanne murmured something unintelligible. She was sitting in the large wingback chair near the window, dozing. Her eyes fluttered open as the door opened.

"Is Melody all right?"

"She'll be OK, but her arm is broken, and her face is a mess. Dennis did a number on her."

"Is she pressing charges?"

"Oh, yes. The police are looking for him now. He must be drunk out of his mind to do something like this." Elizabeth sat wearily on the edge of the bed. "Did Nan get to her hotel all right?"

"Yes. She left about a half hour ago. I told her to go. Nan's a trooper, but she's exhausted too. Do you think—" Ruthanne was interrupted by loud banging on the front door. Elizabeth jumped up, her heart racing with fear. "Who could that be?"

Tom called to them from the hallway. "I've got it. Stay where you are."

A loud male voice rambling on about being sorry rose up the stairs. It sounded like Dennis. Elizabeth reached for the phone to dial 9-1-1. Tom's calm voice instructed Dennis to sit down while he made some coffee. The 9-1-1 operator assured Elizabeth a patrol car would arrive within a few minutes. She wasn't sure if going downstairs would help the situation or further agitate her brother-in-law. Worried for Tom's safety, she tiptoed to the door and opened it carefully. Ruthanne got up from the chair and followed her sister.

"I'm going to the top of stairs," whispered Elizabeth. "Stay here in case you have to call the police again. I hope they hurry."

Ruthanne nodded. Beth tiptoed silently down the hallway, careful to remain out of sight of the first floor when she reached the stairway. "Dear Lord," she prayed, "Don't let Dennis hurt Tom."

Tom's composure remained steady as he kept talking to Dennis. The hiccupping sounds of a man crying came from the kitchen. She heard her husband urge their brother-in-law to drink the coffee.

"She was cheating on me. I know our marriage wasn't perfect, but why did she havta find another guy right away? We're not divorced yet. I don't want a divorce. I was doin' it to make her happy." He swore, and it sounded like a fist pounded the table. "I didn't mean to hurt her. Honest." He began crying again, great gulping sobs.

Elizabeth backed away, trying to decide if she could get to the front door so it would be ready for the police to enter. Holding her breath, she started down the carpeted stairs, hoping that she'd miss the squeaky one and not give herself away. Successful in making it down without a sound, she opened the heavy front door just as two police cars with lights flashing pulled up to the curb. Motioning the officers into the house, she pointed toward the kitchen where the sounds of Dennis' crying were now reduced to some coughing and sniffling. His shoulders slumped, and he put his head on the table when he saw the patrolmen enter the kitchen. He offered no resistance to the handcuffs, looking overwhelmed as he was read his rights.

After the two police officers had finally loaded him into the back of a patrol car, Elizabeth clung to her husband, breathing a prayer of thanks that he was still in one piece. To her surprise, she felt little satisfaction watching Dennis' arrest—mostly grief.

19

hey'd settled the vacation plans on Friday
morning. Everyone was going. God had answered
"yes" to another prayer. The sisters would be
together. Nan had rented a large SUV so they could all
ride in comfort. Nan had also appointed herself the
designated driver, since letting anyone else in the
driver's seat drove her crazy. It was a control thing—an
idiosyncrasy, but as Ruthanne pointed out, it was
honest. It suited them fine, anyway. Melody couldn't
drive, Beth didn't care to drive further than Rochester,
and Ruthanne could nap.

Melody had informed them she would collect
disability while she was off from work. She already had
two weeks of vacation time on the books, which she was
taking first. Considering that Dennis was already out on
bail, the further from Sheffield she was, the better, they
all felt. A restraining order was in place against her
soon-to-be ex-husband, who wasn't supposed to get
within a quarter mile of her. Her face was now three
shades of colors—gray-blue, pink, and yellow. At least
the swollen eye was almost normal, Ruthanne observed.

The excitement of the trip reminded Ruthanne of
their family loading up the Plymouth station wagon

back when they were young. Melody was rattling on about the beach and shopping. Beth was talking about whale watching, restaurants, and art galleries. Ruthanne looked at her mother's drawings every day, burning the image of the young girl into her brain. She would be a grown woman–30 years old. Her daughter was probably married and had a family, which meant that Ruthanne could be a grandmother. The thought was thrilling and frightening all at once. And what if her daughter didn't want to meet her, to know her? That was the most frightening of all.

Ruthanne had slept restlessly, dreaming intermittently of the beach.

There was no one there except for the gulls overhead. She searched for the young girl and only found small footprints that led to the dunes. A figure headed toward her, a mere speck, but she could tell it was a man. She turned and ran, feet flailing in the hot sand. It seemed to suck her in like grains running through an hourglass. A dark-haired woman sat drawing on a large sketch pad. She laughed at Ruthanne's attempts to escape and kept drawing.

An early morning thunderstorm washed the roads clean for their departure. Nan was a firm believer in the earlier on the road, the earlier you get there, and the earlier you start having fun. Clara and Emma gave them sleepy goodbye hugs, while Matthew stood sucking his thumb, pulling it out to ask for Cheerios every few seconds. Tom gave Beth a long kiss, which drew applause from everyone and a blush from his surprised wife. He wasn't usually so demonstrative in public. With the luggage finally jammed into the back of the SUV, Nan gave the two-minute warning.

"Y'all better get in because this here bus is pullin' out. The driver is not known for dilly-dallyin' around."

Ruthanne grinned and shook her head. Nan was using her principal voice, which was effective in getting them in the vehicle. Obediently they climbed in, slammed the doors, and waved to the Hartman family on the sidewalk.

It was dark when they rolled into the driveway of 1612 Sea Urchin Way. A dim porch light was on next to the front door. Melody was sound asleep after taking a pain pill two hours earlier. A pillow propped up her cast against the window. She groaned and yawned as Nan slid the vehicle into park.

"Here we are, ladies. Safe and sound. Let's hope the key is under the mat."

"You don't have a key?" Beth stirred from dozing, suddenly wide awake. "What will we do at this hour?"

"Nan is a kidder, Beth." Ruthanne stretched her arms overhead, turning side to side to loosen up her stiff muscles. "I'm sure she has a key."

"Actually, it's supposed to be under the mat. It's kind of a casual arrangement here." She got out and plodded up the steps. She bent down and moments later held up a key. "Here it is," she said brightly. "Let's go to bed."

The Time Under Heaven

Beth was the first one down to the kitchen in the morning. They'd only made a quick tour of the house last night. They were all tired from the 12-hour road trip. The old-fashioned New England farm kitchen had been replaced by a state-of-the-art gourmet kitchen with a huge hood and indoor grill. The countertops were black granite with cherry cabinetry. She had to admit that Grandma would have killed to cook in a kitchen like this. She hoped there was some coffee stashed away, so she could at least get some caffeine before they made a shopping trip. Once she started opening cupboards, she found they were fully stocked with canned goods. There were plenty of pots, pans, and dishes. There were two coffee makers, one of which was the one-cup type that used tiny containers of specialty coffee. A carousel of coffees sat next to it. Looking into the stainless steel French door refrigerator, she found it full of fresh vegetables, fruit, milk, cheese—everything. Since Nan had done the hard work all day yesterday, Beth thought the least she could do was make breakfast for everyone. Pulling out eggs, milk, cheese, and bread, she decided on cheese omelets to start the day. A knock at the kitchen door startled her. She could see a young woman with indistinct features through the lacy curtain that hung on the window.

"Yes?" she said as she opened the door.

"Hi. I'm Stephanie. I'm the housekeeper and cook."

"Really?" Elizabeth let her in. Nan certainly didn't do anything halfway. "Uh, I guess I wasn't aware that we had a housekeeper." She felt like an awkward, unsophisticated country bumpkin.

"Oh, I'm sorry. I should have left a note when I was stocking the kitchen yesterday."

She was thin and a little taller than Beth, with straight dark hair that hung past the middle of her back. It swayed like blackstrap molasses as she walked to the island, looking at the assortment of groceries Beth had just put there. Her eyes were icy-blue, fringed with thick dark lashes. Not quite pretty, but striking, Beth thought.

"That's all right. I was just going to make coffee and omelets this morning. I don't mind."

"I'd be happy to make the omelets. What kind does everyone want? I'll make them to order. There's plenty of everything."

"Let me go see if the rest are up yet." She climbed the winding staircase to the second floor. They each had their own bedroom that was decorated in true New England style. Beautifully stitched handmade quilts, four-poster beds, large bureaus, comfortable rocking chairs, and large braided rugs made each room homey and simple. She could hear the shower running in the hall bathroom. Someone was awake. Ruthanne's door was open, and the bed empty. There was no sound from Nan's or Melody's rooms. She decided that a quiet cup of coffee and conversation with Stephanie might be in order this first morning.

An hour later, Melody finally appeared in the kitchen to find her sisters and Nan laughing like teenagers. She stared at Stephanie, who immediately asked her what she'd like for breakfast.

"I don't eat breakfast, just coffee," she muttered, taking a seat on a bench at the large oak trestle table.

"How are you feeling today?" Beth asked. "Any better?" It pained her to look at the bruises on her sister's pretty face.

"Some better, I guess. It's too early to tell yet. I hate the way the pain pills make me feel. I'm going to stick with ibuprofen if I can. I'll miss the whole vacation otherwise." She leaned toward the center of the table and whispered, "Who's the girl?"

"Ah, I forgot to tell y'all that this is a real vacation—no cookin' or cleanin' allowed. Stephanie is our housekeeper. She'll be here to cook breakfast and dinner. Lunches are on our own. Stephanie will make the beds, take care of the laundry, bathrooms, et cetera. No one is to lift a finger or arm as the case may be," Nan smiled at Melody.

"Great! I've never had a vacation like that. In fact, I haven't had a vacation in forever—period, although I wish I could fasten my own bra. I have to ask my big sister for help. Sheesh."

The women all nodded in unison, laughing.

Stephanie placed a cup of coffee in front of Melody. "If you really don't want breakfast, I'll get started upstairs."

"We're finer than frog's hair. Go ahead," Nan told her. "Now, girls, what's the plan of action for today?"

After an extended tour, with the sisters remarking on all the improvements made to Grandma Erickson's house, they walked to the beach. Beth remembered skipping down the sidewalk to the little lane that led down the stairs to the honey-colored beach. Melody wore a huge floppy straw hat and sunglasses to hide the damage to her face. She complained that her tan wouldn't be even with the cast. Beth merely smiled at Ruthanne listening to Mel complain. She must be feeling a little more like her old self. They set up a beach chair for her. Ruthanne arranged a pillow under the cast and then set up her own chair. Beth broke out the sunscreen and bottles of water she'd collected from the kitchen.

"Stay hydrated or you'll end up with wrinkles," she warned, slathering SPF 40 on her arms and legs. "Make sure you get enough sunscreen on too." The last thing any of them needed was skin cancer or sunburn.

Nan and Ruthanne looked at each other and burst out laughing.

"What's so funny?" she demanded.

"We live in Africa, remember?" Ruthanne burbled over Nan's giggle. "We're familiar with the sun."

"Oh... Right."

A light breeze off the sparkling water carried the scent of saltiness. It made her nose tingle, and the urge to walk the familiar beach overcame the urge to sit and read. Besides she'd promised to bring home lots of shells for Matthew and the twins. Announcing her departure, Beth zipped up the white terrycloth cover up and kicked off her sandals. The grit of sand between her toes felt delicious. While the rest read or dozed, Beth let the hypnotic lure of the tide pull her down the beach. When she finally turned to retrace the route back, Ruthanne looked like she was still napping. Melody was reading a magazine, but Nan's chair was empty.

20

Nan waited on the Jacobean print couch in the office of Harold Parker, Esq. The receptionist wore a headset to answer the phone, which rang often. She constantly answered, "Good afternoon, Law Offices." Smooth jazz played in the background. Two other secretaries or paralegals hauled thick files to an office behind the waiting room. The pile of birth certificates she'd ordered from the Hyannis Clerk's Office lay beside her in a manila envelope. Mr. Parker's firm had represented the Erickson family for more than 30 years. It was logical to believe Annaliese had gone to him or one of the other attorneys in the firm to arrange the adoption. She didn't have a lot of hope that Mr. Parker would help her, but it never hurt to ask.

Mr. Parker's office was stuffy and smelled of stale pipe tobacco. He thumbed through the birth certificates, his reading glasses perched on the end of a bulbous nose mapped with tiny red veins spreading to his cheeks. He had a shock of white hair that reminded her of Colonel Sanders. All he needed was a white suit.

"I'm sorry, but I can't help you. Adoption records are sealed, of course. There is a process to open them, but I'm afraid it takes some time. From what you tell me, your friend may not have that time. Plus, it was so long ago." He leaned back in the deep black leather chair and put his arms behind his head, giving Nan a hard look. "I find it curious that you're here without your friend. What's her name?"

"Ruthanne Carroll. Marilyn Erickson's grand-daughter."

"Right. Hmm. I did represent the Ericksons for many years. I handled Marilyn's estate back sometime in the 90s. Her husband was a character. He passed away before Ruthanne was born." He leaned forward, hands pressed against the worn green blotter, a broad smile across his jowly face. He stood and scooped up the birth certificates, shuffling them to stuff back into the envelope.

"Sorry, I can't help you, Mrs. Singleton."

"Singletree," Nan corrected, rising at his cue. "I am indebted to you, sir, for your time," she said, the languid Savannah drawl oozing like honey. She shook his hand and took the envelope.

"You're quite welcome. It's been a pleasure. I wish Ruthanne good luck in finding her daughter." He rubbed the back of his neck and opened the door for her. "She was a brave young woman. I imagine she's still the same if she's dealing with cancer and this search."

Nan studied his inscrutable dark brown eyes. She smiled brilliantly and said, "She sure is. Thank you. Y'all have a nice day."

The sisters and Nan sat on the front porch while Stephanie finished cleaning the kitchen before leaving for the evening. The dinner of grilled sea bass and steamed fresh vegetables had been pronounced perfection. The small talk tapered off, and Nan looked at Ruthanne.

"Are you two conspiring?" Beth asked.

Ruthanne recognized the hint of jealousy in her sister's voice and shook her head. "Nan's giving me the high sign that I need to talk about my search."

"I wondered when you were going to get around to it," Melody said, adjusting her position in the Adirondack chair. Her legs were stretched out on the matching ottoman. "We've talked my situation to death," she said, giving Beth a hard look and an arched eyebrow.

"Just trying to give you some sisterly advice," Beth countered mildly.

"I'm not stupid. I wouldn't go back to him for love or money!" Melody snapped.

The screen door squeaked as it swung out. Stephanie stepped onto the porch. She wore khaki-colored Bermudas with a peacock-blue print tank top. Her hair was pulled back into a loose bun.

"I'll see you ladies in the morning, unless there's something else you need."

"We're dandy," Nan said. "There is one thing. Have you lived around here for long?"

"All my life."

"Do you remember Mrs. Erickson who used to live here before the Braydens bought the house?"

"Sure. She was a nice old lady. Always working in her flower gardens. My family lived just three houses down."

Ruthanne leaned forward in her chair. "Is your family still here?"

"My parents are, but my brother and sister are in Boston. Not enough going on here for them. I don't mind though. I like it."

Ruthanne quickly guessed that Stephanie was probably about Corinne's age, so she wouldn't have known someone who was now 30, but her parents just might.

"Mrs. Erickson was our grandmother," Melody burst out. "We stayed here every summer for years."

"Really," Stephanie said. "I had no idea. Wow! It must be weird to be staying here now."

"A little," Beth said, plunging into the conversation. "The house looks really nice though. Are your parents still down the street?"

Ruthanne guessed that Beth had the same thought about Stephanie's parents.

"No. They're in Barnstable." She looked at her watch. "Sorry, but I'd better get going. I'm taking some online courses, and I need to get a paper done tonight."

"Of course, we don't want to hold you up," Ruthanne said.

"Good night, then. I'll be back in the morning."

Ruthanne watched the young woman ride off on the bicycle she'd left by the tiny potting shed next to the driveway.

"We should talk to her parents. They may remember when you were here, Ruthanne." Beth's voice had a tremor of excitement.

"Maybe," Ruthanne replied. "But I want to start at the high school tomorrow. I think I'll go alone and let the rest of you shop or go to the beach. This is a vacation after all."

"I thought you wanted our help,'" Melody protested.

"I do. As much as I want to find my daughter, there's a part of me that's terrified."

"I always thought you were the bravest person ever. You went to Africa by yourself. You've lived with...well, primitive people for years."

Ruthanne smiled at the pride she saw shine from her little sister's eyes. Too bad it was misplaced.

"It doesn't take a lot of courage to run. And that's what I've been doing for a long time."

Ruthanne leaned back in the rocking chair and closed her eyes. "I'm tired of running."

"Running from having an illegitimate child? Running from giving her up for adoption?"

Ruthanne opened her eyes and looked at Beth. Her harsh tone surprised and wounded her. It took her a moment to recover and smooth the defensive hackles.

"All of the above and more," she replied evenly. "I think we all have things we avoid or run from. Don't you?"

"I know that's true for a fact," Nan interjected. "All of us have a few skeletons in the closet, and it's only the good Lord's forgiveness and grace that helps us toss 'em out in the trash."

"I've always tried to face things head on and deal with life as it comes," Beth said. "I've tried to make good decisions…"

"Head on? Really? Come on, Beth, what about this thing with Corinne?" Melody shifted her position on the chair, carefully lifting her cast to avoid hitting the armrest on the chair.

"Most of that situation is not my decision. I did try to call her, but she wasn't working the day that I did."

"You tried calling Corinne?" Ruthanne asked, surprised. "You didn't say anything about it."

"I didn't talk to her, so I didn't mention it."

"Have you tried again? I have Rick and Leah's number. They could let you know how she is."

"I thought about it, but I was…"

"Afraid," Melody finished for her. "That's why I left the church. Christians are all hypocrites. Always telling other people how they should act, but when it comes to themselves, it's a different story." She slid forward in the chair and twisted to get up. "I'm going to bed. I'll see you in the morning. Don't wake me up again either."

The three women sat in silence until they heard Melody start up the stairs. Beth huffed in irritation.

"It's always the same with Mel. It's everyone else, but never her."

"Self-preservation. We're all guilty as charged," Nan chuckled.

"I think you should try calling Corinne again," Ruthanne said. "There's no harm in that."

"I *am* afraid. Mel's right. What if she refuses to speak to me? I don't think I could handle that."

The darkness enfolded the porch, and a few mosquitoes began high-pitched humming. Nan grabbed the can of bug repellent and sprayed around their chairs.

"I don't think that would happen. She may be waiting for you to make the first contact." Ruthanne took the repellent and quickly sprayed her arms. "Fear keeps us stationary and keeps us from doing the right thing. I understand how you feel. He hasn't given us a spirit of fear." She paused, realizing that her comments sounded preachy.

"Maybe." Beth fell silent, looking at the sky twinkling with stars. The blinking lights of a jet streaked through the night. "You're probably right. I'm just wasting time when I could be doing something to fix the situation." She rose and put her hand on Ruthanne's shoulder. "I'm sorry, Ruthie."

21

A large copier behind the two desks was spitting out booklets every few minutes as it churned paper. Ruthanne wrinkled her nose. The indefinable school smell was there made up of paper, pencils, and probably dirty gym clothes permeating the very walls. The secretary brought out a pile of yearbooks and dumped them on the counter.

"If you want to use the desk over there," the short gray-haired woman jabbed a thumb toward a cluttered desk, "you can. Michelle's on vacation."

"Thank you. I will." Ruthanne scooped up the books of varying colors and made herself comfortable in the armless desk chair. She pulled the picture of the fourteen-year-old from the portfolio. Flipping open the first book from '95, she began searching through the freshman class pictures. There were lots of dark-haired girls, but none who looked like the drawing. She turned back to the eighth grade class and met with the same results. The faces in the homeroom pictures were difficult to pick out. She'd always hated those pictures. Everyone was smushed together like cattle. You usually stood next to someone who had too much perfume or not enough deodorant. Just to be certain, Ruthanne scanned through the rest of the yearbook. She wasn't there. For the next hour, she carefully examined four different yearbooks. The results were the same. Sighing, she restacked them and placed them on the counter. The secretary was on the phone, writing a message on a pink pad. When she finally looked up, Ruthanne gave her a smile.

"Thanks for letting me look through these."

"Any luck?" She looked over her reading glasses at Ruthanne.

"No. But I was wondering if you'd look at a drawing I have and tell me if you recognize the girl."

The secretary made her way to the counter.

"Nice drawing. Did you do this?"

"Oh, no. My mother was the artist. She loved to draw."

The woman shook her head. "She doesn't look familiar to me. This was in 1995, right?"

"Yes. This would have been drawn in the summer."

"That was a long time ago. I see so many kids come through here. She's a striking girl. Why are you looking for her?"

Ruthanne shifted uneasily, unsure of what she should share. "She's a family member that we've lost track of. She was adopted, so I don't have a name."

"Oh." A shadow of suspicion crossed the secretary's eyes. "Your mother didn't know her name?"

"I don't know. She never said. My mother grew up here. She was Annaliese Erickson."

"Erickson," the woman murmured. "I remember some Ericksons. A couple of boys with that last name were in school ahead of me, I think."

"Probably my uncles. Peter and Stan."

"Sounds right. They were good athletes. One of them was in trouble a lot," she said, smiling.

"That would be my Uncle Pete. He's a practical joker." Her mother's younger brothers were cut-ups. Both traveled from Boston when the Carrolls vacationed at the Cape to visit. Parties at Grandma's house were raucous, with her mother playing the piano, Uncle Pete on the guitar, and Uncle Stan with makeshift drums made from buckets and coffee cans. They sang and played everything from "You are My Sunshine," to "I'll Fly Away," to "Shortenin' Bread." Her father usually left to study about halfway through their concerts.

"Have you tried The Dunes?" the secretary said, tapping her forehead, "It's a private school, K through 12."

"No. I didn't know there was one here."

"Oh, yes. For years. You might have better luck there. It's a little persnickety, but I know the headmaster's secretary. I could give her a call if you want."

"Would you? I'd appreciate that."

The winding driveway to The Dunes was edged with brick in a herringbone pattern. Well-placed groves of pine trees were like football huddles scattered across the broad lawn that led to an impressive red brick façade with white trim. Tall, arched windows stood like sentries at the front of the building. Rambling, waxy-leaved rhododendrons flanked the brick below the windows. Massive stone urns filled with red, white, and purple-blue petunias sat at the bottom of the steps leading to the entrance. This was old New England—formal, stately, intimidating. A bronze directory on a marble pedestal indicated that the main building housed the headmaster, dean of students, and the administrative offices.

Steeling herself for more disappointment, Ruthanne placed her hand on the door. Were schools the best place to look? Should she start somewhere else? She glanced at the slip of paper the high school secretary had given her. The name written on the paper was Eva Hall, who was expecting her. Tentatively pushing the door open, she entered a large foyer with hallways connecting to it on the left and right. Straight through the foyer was another hallway with white columns that ran from floor to ceiling. The sign to the right pointed the way to the headmaster, the dean, and the administrative offices. Hardwood floors gleamed, and an intricately designed runner, obviously expensive and Persian, led down the hallway. Ceramic pots of varying colors held ferns that graced rosewood accent tables. The tables with their scrollwork legs and piecrust tops gave the hallway a Victorian feel.

The atmosphere made her feel underdressed in the simple blue print sundress with its loose matching belt. She nervously ruffled her short hair, and then smoothed it, hoping she was presentable. An elegant grandfather clock intoned the half hour, making her heart race as she walked down the hallway. The office was through the first doorway. Cheerful sunlight and the immaculately manicured side lawns were visible from two large windows. A low counter met a higher one, forming a right angle. The wood was dark and aged. Classical music filled the background pleasantly while a laser printer whirred letters into the tray. A white-haired woman with gold-framed glasses looked up over the low counter and smiled.

"You must be Ms. Carroll."

"Yes, that's right. You must be Mrs. Hall." She felt immediately at ease, her heart slowing to a more normal rate. "I'm doing some family research, and I was hoping to look through some of your yearbooks."

"We have yearbooks back to 1875. Where would you like to begin?"

Ruthanne laughed and then caught herself. It seemed out of place here. "Uh, not quite that far back. Maybe starting with 1994 and 1995."

"No problem. Do you know the name of the student? I've been here for 35 years. I may know whoever it is you're looking for."

"That's a bit of a mystery. I don't have a name, but I do have a drawing of her. Would you like to take a look at it?"

"I'd be happy to. Come on in and have a seat." She unlatched the gate that kept unauthorized students from going behind the counter. Ruthanne sat down in a comfortable chair by an executive-quality desk. She unzipped the portfolio and pulled out the pictures dated '94 and '95. The one from '94 was of the girl eating a hotdog and drink at a picnic table. Lanky hair half-hid her face, and her legs were drawn up on the bench.

"These are very nice. Did you draw them?"

"No. My mother was the artist. I can't draw a straight line myself."

Eva looked closely at the drawings and leaned back in her chair. "She looks very familiar. When was this?"

"In 1994 and '95. She was 13 and 14 in these pictures."

"An eighth or ninth grader..." Eva's voice trailed off. She rose from the chair and went to an antique bookcase with glass doors. It was filled with thin hardback yearbooks. They were mostly black with gold lettering. Ruthanne allowed a bubble of hope to surface.

"Let me see," Eva said cracking open the first yearbook entitled *The Legend*, laying it flat on her desk. "There was a girl I seem to remember who was here for a year or two." She suddenly stopped, her face blanched. "Maybe not."

"Is something wrong? I do want to find out her name and something about her."

"Well, I guess it wouldn't be any secret. There was an accident in the summer of 1995 during a special summer session here. A girl drowned in one of the ponds on campus. It was a terrible thing."

Ruthanne felt her stomach sink, and an ache came to her throat. "Is her picture in the yearbook?"

"I believe so," Eva said quietly as she turned to the freshman class picture. "I can't remember her first name, but her last name was Wilcox. Here she is," she said pointing to a wistful-looking, dark-haired teenager. "That's right," Eva said underscoring the picture with her finger "Her name was Samantha Wilcox. Everyone called her Sammie. A little bit wild, but a good girl. The accident was such a shame."

Ruthanne gazed at the face staring out from the black and white pages. She certainly bore a resemblance to the girl in her mother's drawing. Could she be sure that Mama had only drawn her daughter? Maybe she had taken up drawing random young girls on the beach. The thought plummeted the bit of hope she'd felt only minutes earlier. This girl was gone. The road ended with a picture in a yearbook. Was this what she was supposed to find out? She shook her head slowly in disbelief.

"Do you mind if I look through the rest of these pictures?"

"No. Not at all. You can take a seat at the work table in the back if you'd like."

Ruthanne took the books and settled in at a long table stacked with textbooks on one end. The sunlight filtered through the pines that partially blocked the view to the driveway. She watched a sparrow perched on the windowsill peer in at her before flying away. Matthew 10:29 immediately rushed into her mind.

The Time Under Heaven

Are not two sparrows sold for a penny?
Yet not one of them will fall to the ground apart from the
will of Your Father.

Was her daughter the sparrow that had fallen to the ground? Was the Father letting her know this now?

She closed her eyes, offering a silent prayer: "Father, you know everything. Does my search end here? Is she the one? I pray that it isn't the end. Please comfort Samantha's family, who must still miss her."

She opened the yearbook and began searching the faces of the 15 girls in the 1994 eighth grade class. Only Samantha's features were similar to the drawing. Her nose was thin and straight. Her eyebrows were arched over wide set dark eyes with thick lashes. The eyes in her mother's drawings were always lighter—gray, the color of Danny's. She couldn't be the one, could she? Uncertain, Ruthanne turned back to look at the other girls again. No one came close to her mother's drawings. She took another yearbook from the stack and found the freshman class. Eva was correct. An in memoriam page had been given to Samantha Jane Wilcox. The dates read June 26, 1981 – July 23, 1995.

Her hands trembled. It wasn't her daughter. The birth date was wrong. Her mother had drawn the last picture in August of 1995, much later than Samantha's death. The picture wasn't of Samantha Wilcox. She willed herself to turn the page.

22

Beth and Melody strolled down the bustling sidewalks filled with summer tourists. Parents with overtired children, sullen teens, and a few elderly couples went in and out of candy shops, galleries, antique shops, and the rest of the assortment that made up Wellfleet. They had stopped for lunch at The Bean Pot, where hearty fare was popular. They'd ordered lobster salads that came with cornbread shaped like ears of corn. Now they were walking off lunch and window shopping. Nan was spending the day at the house, ostensibly to catch up on emails from the Academy.

"Let's check out this antique shop," Beth said, taking in the window display of Amy's Antiques.

"All right," Melody agreed. Her interest was in the designer clothing shops across the street. The price tags were far more than she ever spent on clothes, but a splurge was in order after what she'd been through in the last week, she reasoned. The cast was beginning to itch, and she wished for a pencil to slide through the narrow opening to take care of the problem.

The musty smell of old upholstery and beeswax greeted them when Beth pushed the door open. A little bell jangled merrily, announcing their arrival. The shop was gloomy after the bright sunlight outside. Beth headed for a display of teacups, while Melody wandered over to a black velvet board pinned with old brooches and necklaces. The prices made it obvious the pieces were costume jewelry, although one necklace caught her eye. It looked like an amethyst. It was in a silver teardrop setting with tiny diamonds around it. She fingered it and noticed a white-haired man with a distinct stoop crossing to her, a pleasant smile on his face. His eyes crinkled with good humor behind his glasses.

"Good afternoon, young lady. See anything you like?"

Melody smiled back. "This is a very pretty necklace," she said, pointing at the pendant. "I don't see a price tag though."

"A-ah," he said in typical New England fashion. "It's probably fallen off." He rummaged around behind the velvet board without success. Beth appeared with a cup and saucer decorated in yellow roses.

"Did you find something you like, Mel?"

"I thought this necklace was really pretty. It actually reminds me of a necklace Grandma wore. He's looking for a price tag right now."

"It is pretty. I'm not sure I remember Grandma having a necklace like this. It's your favorite color though."

"That's what caught my eye, of course." Melody smiled, remembering how she'd insisted on everything being lavender in her bedroom when she was in high school. The walls, the bedspread, the sheets, everything was lavender. Mama had finally given in to the monochromatic décor choice.

"Of course. Do you have any idea what you want for it?" she asked the elderly man, who had lifted the excess black velvet fabric that draped the table before carefully laying it down again. He looked up, the smile still on his face. His gnarled hands gently lifted the necklace from the pins that held up the fine silver chain.

"Well, it's been here quite awhile, and since it reminds you of your Grandma and all, I think you should have it. Consider it a serendipitous gift."

Melody's eyes widened in surprise. "I couldn't do that. That wouldn't be right," she answered, struggling to regain some composure. Either the old man was not all there, or he was setting her up for some sort of catch.

"It's something I want to do," he said fumbling with the tiny clasp. "My hands aren't quite as nimble as they used to be." He handed it to Elizabeth, who quickly put the teacup on the table and took the necklace. "I was given a great gift many years ago. I thought I should be able to pay for it, but I couldn't. It was way beyond my price range. When I accepted the gift, it's made all the difference. Gift giving is something I like to do these days, following a great example."

Now she eyed the man with outright suspicion. What exactly was he up to? "Really, it's not right. I'm happy to pay for it." She stepped back from her sister, who held the necklace, ready to put it around her neck. Why wouldn't he just set a price?

"It's without a price," he said gently. "It can only be received as a gift."

"I can't. Really. Beth, I can't take this," she looked for some sort of support from Beth. Her sister had dropped her hands. The necklace dangled from her fingers. The situation was way too strange. She needed to get out of the shop. "My arm is really starting to hurt again. I need to go back to the house."

"All right. Let me pay for this cup and saucer. I'll meet you outside." Beth was abrupt, turning toward the cash register.

Melody hurried from the shop and back onto the street, a curious sensation coming over her—one from the past. The words the man had spoken were all too familiar. How many times had she heard her father say that salvation was a gift? That it was without price? Was that what the old man was getting at, or was she off base? Maybe it was the pain meds. They might be messing with her perception or something. The milling pedestrian traffic moved her toward the fudge shop next door. The smells were enticing. Glancing at the vast selection of candy in the window, she decided that Beth would probably preach at her the whole way back to the house. It might even be a setup. She watched Beth talk to the man as she pulled cash from her wallet and hand it to him at the old-fashioned register. They seemed pretty chummy. Melody decided to start the long walk back to the house alone. She wasn't up to conversation.

Ruthanne sat staring at the pile of drawings and the stack of yearbooks. What was she thinking? The task was impossible. No faces popped out from the yearbooks to match her mother's artwork. What if these weren't of her daughter? They may have been of a girl that Mama thought was her granddaughter. Or maybe the girl lived somewhere else and just vacationed at the Cape. She rested her chin on her hands, feeling a wave of fatigue come in like the tide. Her emotions were on a roller coaster ride, and it was taking a toll. Ruthanne glanced at her watch—2:30. A nap should have been her only occupation for the afternoon. She'd even forgotten about lunch.

Sighing, she stowed the pictures back into the portfolio. With a quick thank you to Eva Hall, she trudged back to the SUV. If she didn't get back to the house soon, she'd be asleep on her feet. Heat rolled out of the vehicle, and the steering wheel burned her hands. A fiery trial—was that what she was going through? Wasn't the cancer enough? But trials weren't supposed to be easy, that's why they were trials.

The ignition turned over instantly; the AC blew hot and then cool air on her face. "...the testing of your faith develops perseverance." The book of James was cropping up again. The brother of Jesus knew how to meddle, she thought grimly. He also said to "count it pure joy" when trials came along. A longing for the steady slow pulse of the Maasai village life overwhelmed her. If she could only sit down and have a cup of tea with her friends there.

Elizabeth wasn't surprised to find herself walking back to the house without Melody. It never failed. Anytime she was confronted with spiritual truth, Melody ran. How could her sister continue to reject it? They'd all been raised the same way. Daddy had been strict, but he'd loved them. They all knew that without question. And now a complete stranger talks to Mel—it had to be a God thing. What a strange encounter, but refreshing. Impulsively, she pulled her cell phone from a small straw purse and considered calling Corinne. There was time. Ruthanne had been right about fear. It was paralyzing her. She was now on a quiet side street three blocks from the house. The shade of the trees had cooled the temperatures here. Elizabeth pulled her damp blouse away from her waist. A slight breeze ruffled the leaves, bringing some relief.

She was really out of shape. The doctor had told her regular walking would help with her blood pressure and weight. Who had time? She stopped and hit the contacts button, scrolling through the numbers until she found the deli. Her index finger was poised over the send button. Perspiration reappeared on her upper lip. Last week's Sunday School lesson shot from her brain to the hesitant finger. *"Above all, love each other deeply, because love covers over a multitude of sins."*

23

Dinner was a quiet affair. The day had been disappointing for everyone, except Nan. She'd proudly announced she'd answered all the emails electronically stacked in her inbox.

"Sounds like everything is running like a well-oiled machine," Ruthanne commented.

"It is. It is. The registrar emailed me that enrollment numbers for September are excellent. Charlie, that's my assistant headmaster, is pleased as punch to have hired a new school nurse. She's Scottish, which has got to be a pleasant change from Nurse Anika."

"Why's that?" Melody questioned.

Nan snorted. "The woman did not like children. Why she applied in the first place is beyond me. Her credentials were sparklin' though, and I hired her. It was a big mistake. She told me halfway through last school year that Nairobi was far too hot and dirty for her. The shopping wasn't up to snuff either. Jumping Jehoshaphat! The woman was the absolute limit. I ask for two-year commitments from most of my staff and faculty, but I was more than happy to release her. She was on a plane back to Denmark in July."

There was polite laughter around the table.

"Any takers for a game of Scrabble tonight?" suggested Nan.

A murmur of "no thanks" went around the table. Beth glanced at her cell phone, which lay next to her plate. Ruthanne stirred the pile of mashed potatoes with her fork like she was mixing up a batch of cookies. Her appetite was non-existent tonight even though the dinner looked and smelled wonderful.

"Ladies, I'm retirin' early tonight," Nan said pushing back from the table. "I believe y'all need some family time." Without further comment, she left the dining room. Beth's puzzled face turned to Ruthanne, who was intently refolding her linen napkin.

"Did we insult Nan or something?"

Ruthanne sighed and shook her head. "She's right. Can't you feel the tension between us?"

"Tension? I don't think that's true."

"Beth, really?" Melody pushed back her chair and strode toward the front porch, elevating her broken arm to chest height.

"Let's have coffee on the porch, Beth," Ruthanne urged. "We need to talk." Maybe they could get all of their issues out into the open. She didn't want to spend the rest of their time walking on eggshells with each other. It would be a miserable vacation if that happened.

Beth raised her eyebrows and sniffed. "I'll get a tray from Stephanie."

The sun was sliding down behind the pines at the back of the house; the front porch was already immersed in twilight. Ruthanne lit three small buckets of citronella, blowing out the wooden match and placing it beside the middle candle. Melody sat on the Adirondack love seat, her feet resting on a corner of the square coffee table. When Elizabeth appeared with a tray of steaming mugs, Melody dropped her feet to the floor.

"Here we are," she said with forced cheerfulness. Elizabeth took her cell phone from the tray and placed it on the table near her chair. Melody gave her a sideways look, grabbed the thick handle of the closest mug, and took a sip.

Ruthanne put her hands around a hot mug. Even though the evening was warm and still, a chill had crept into her bones. She'd slept for two hours since coming back from the school, but fatigue was still sapping her energy. Her thoughts were disjointed, but there were things she needed to say. She prayed that she could put the sentences together. Maybe the whole trip had been a mistake, but they were here.

She began with a favorite memory when she was ten and had been allowed to stay here by herself for two whole days during their vacation. Grandma had taught her to make bread; Uncle Peter and Uncle Stan had taken her out to the beach to dig for clams and to fish. They'd made a campfire on the beach, broiling their catch over the open flame and baking the clams in the coals of the fire. They ate with their fingers, got messy, and then ran into the ocean to wash off.

"I did that when I was ten, too," Melody laughed. "My bread was as hard as a rock. Grandma's was perfect of course. Then the uncles took me sailing."

"It was Grandma's grown-up vacation when you reached double digits," Beth smiled, her eyes crinkling with humor. "I made sweet rolls that I sprinkled with paprika instead of cinnamon."

"Oooh, yuck!" Melody exclaimed. They all laughed, chattering about their baking disasters.

"Grandma always did something special with us," Ruthanne agreed. "It's so strange to be in this house without her here."

"Everything is so different it doesn't feel like her house anymore," Beth pondered.

"But it's still Grandma's house. I'm sleeping in her bedroom," Melody responded. "It's a little weird, even though it's been redecorated. I feel like she's here."

"It was always the one place we could relax, be ourselves," Ruthanne hesitated, not sure she should continue.

"No kidding! No church people trying to catch us doing something wrong so they could tell Daddy. Mama could draw and not work so hard, always cooking and cleaning. Grandma did all of it for her." Melody took another sip of the cooling coffee, a faraway look in her eyes.

"When Uncle Pete and Uncle Stan had families, it was even more fun with cousins. They were little, but so cute," Beth added. "It's sad we haven't kept in touch. After Grandma died, we all drifted apart."

"Kind of like us," Ruthanne jumped in at the opening. "We've all done our own thing for a long time. That's one of the reasons I wanted us to go on this trip. Really get to know each other again."

"Well, maybe for you," Melody said. "You're always away. Beth and I see each other all the time."

Beth squirmed in the chair, a frown creasing her mouth. "We see each other, but we don't."

"What's that supposed to mean?" Melody's tone was sharp.

"Nothing."

Melody's face turned sulky. She concentrated on the red-haired woman walking a shaggy collie down the sidewalk.

"What I mean is that we don't do things together, like go shopping or have lunch. It's well...um...except for lately." Beth regained her composure. "Since you've been home, Ruthanne, we've had a lot of family time. It's been good."

Melody's face relaxed. "You're right, I guess. I'm always working because I have to. Dennis couldn't keep a job. Construction is way down. We were always scraping by. At least I won't have to worry about that anymore, unless he decides to come after me again." She rubbed the cast.

"And we're so glad that you're getting better, Ruthanne. We do need this time together. We didn't have nearly enough after Mama died. It was all so fast, and you went back...almost like you couldn't wait to get away from us." Beth's voice was reproving.

"Actually, I was and have been." Ruthanne replied. She might as well be brutally honest. All of this was her doing anyway.

"Sheesh! We're *that* awful?" Melody leaned forward in the chair to get comfortable. She gingerly lowered the injured arm to her body.

"It wasn't you or Beth. It was me. I've been running from...well, a lot of things. Mostly the fact that I had a child out of wedlock. I was terrified for years that I'd be found out."

"Why? We all screw up. Everybody knows I have. Look at me." Melody raised her broken arm and turned her bruised face toward Ruthanne. "I married an idiot."

Beth looked away, her face impassive in deepening twilight. "I didn't. I married a good man. We've had a good life, except for this thing with..." Her voice broke, and she cleared her throat. "The thing with Corinne." She sighed heavily. "Mel's right. We all mess up; no matter how hard we try to do the right thing." She turned back to her sisters. "I guess I've been so angry with Tom that I've..." Her voice trailed off. The cell phone on the coffee table chimed out a tinkling piano melody. Elizabeth snatched the phone, peering at the caller ID in the darkness. "Sorry. I have to take this," she said rising from the chair. Crossing the porch, they heard the screen door shut as she answered the call.

"I'll bet it's Corinne," Melody said. "Beth is really over the edge about that situation. They've kept such a tight leash on that girl; I'm surprised this didn't happen before. Everybody needs to get some of that wild oats out of their system. I did. You did. Beth is a little too tightly wound. But she always has been."

Ruthanne closed her eyes. Melody was still fighting their father in some ways. Rebellion was her badge of honor.

"We've all done things we regret. I really wish I hadn't fallen for Danny. It would have saved me a lot of grief. And others too."

"You ended up being a missionary. A lot of good came out of it, right?" Melody stood and went to the porch railing. She traced the fingers of her left hand over the smooth white wood.

"I took the hard way to the mission field and hauled a lot of baggage with me." Ruthanne stretched her legs and re-crossed her ankles.

"But now you'll find your daughter. I know you will. You're getting a second chance with the cancer. It's all working out. Like for me. Once the divorce is final, I've decided I'm moving. I can finally do whatever I want."

"Where does God fit into this picture?" It suddenly occurred to her that she'd hardly ever had any sort of spiritual conversation with her youngest sister. Not in a very long time, at least.

"I'm not sure why He should fit into my picture. He's never been much interested in me, and honestly I haven't been impressed with Him. We make our own way. You dug yourself out of a mess, and I'm digging my way out too." She turned around to face Ruthanne, leaning against the railing.

Ruthanne's heart sank. The answer stung.

"He's very much interested in you, Mel. And nobody can dig themselves out. Not really."

"You couldn't prove it by me," she said with a toss of her head, walking to the door.

She stopped short as Beth appeared in the doorway, the light from the living room backlighting her face. Her brown eyes were dark with worry.

"Leah just called me about Corinne. I think I'm going to have to leave."

24

Elizabeth paced between the large bay window and the conversation area while her sisters took seats in the overstuffed furniture. She finally sat on the edge of the window seat cushion, perched like a hawk ready to strike its prey. She rubbed her hands together nervously. It was taking every ounce of willpower to stay reasonably calm.

In a measured voice, Beth explained that she'd worked up enough courage to call the deli again, but when she'd finally gotten through, the waitress who answered informed her Corinne didn't work there anymore. A quick call to Leah had made her more concerned because the couple hadn't been able to contact Corinne in several days. Leah had confirmed to Beth in the last call that Corinne and Trevor were no longer in the tiny room they rented three blocks from the deli. Rick was checking a nearby homeless shelter to try and locate the pair.

"I'd like to rent a car and get to New York tomorrow. It's just a few hours away. I hate to do this, but I'm really concerned."

"Of course. Have you called Tom?" Ruthanne asked.

"No. I'm not sure if I should. I don't want him to tell me not to go. I need to do this."

"Why would he say no?"

Beth sighed. She should call Tom. He couldn't stop her from going, but she didn't want another confrontation about Corinne. But something could be really wrong, and he should know.

"I'll call," she said with resignation.

"Where do you think they would go?" Melody asked, picking at the upholstery of the chair with her good hand.

"I have no idea. Until Ruthanne met up with her, we didn't know exactly where she was in New York. I wish I could talk to her." She rubbed her temples, willing the ache in her head to disappear.

"I think we should go with you," Ruthanne said firmly. "Or at least I'll go if Melody isn't up to it. I don't think you should go by yourself."

"Sure. I'm OK with it. It's probably a good idea. You'll need someone to navigate once we get to the city," Melody responded eagerly. "I haven't been to New York since high school. I'd love to see it again."

"That's OK. I can do this alone. This is your trip, Ruthanne. You've just started your search. I couldn't ask you to do this."

"It will wait a few more days. Nan can enjoy some time on her own. She won't mind."

"Nan won't mind what?" Nan entered the living room in a voluminous pink-striped terrycloth robe, reading glasses perched on her head. A manila envelope was in her hand.

Ruthanne updated Nan on Beth's plans. Without comment, Nan walked to the coffee table and spilled the contents of the envelope. Copies of birth certificates scattered across the well-polished cherry surface.

"What are you doing?" Melody asked with annoyance.

"A trip to New York is just what I was goin' to suggest myself," Nan said, lowering her full figure onto the loveseat next to Melody. "Let me show y'all what I found."

25

A warm breeze fluttered through the curtains that covered the front windows. The bracing smell of the ocean drifted into the living room and pushed the papers toward the back edge. Elizabeth rose to look at the jumble strewn across the coffee table. Melody sat forward, resting her cast on the arm of the loveseat. Nan held the top copy out to Ruthanne, who stood by the table. She looked questioningly at her friend.

"This is the one," she said with satisfaction.

"What do you mean? H-hh-how...?" Ruthanne stammered, looking down at the birth certificate.

"Now, Mr. Parker, Esquire wasn't much help the day of our meetin', or so I thought, but he was in fact, *very* helpful. Do you see the corners?" She pointed to the top left and then to the bottom right.

"They're folded," Elizabeth said.

"Exactly," Nan beamed. "They were not folded when I gave them to Mr. Parker. These were folded deliberately. I hadn't taken them out of the envelope since I met with him until tonight." Her round face was red with excitement, her brown eyes dancing.

Ruthanne took the certificate and fingered the edges. She quickly scanned for the name—Audrey Anne

Wright. The baby had been born on May 24, 1981 at 5:21 p. m. and weighed six pounds, three ounces. She'd given birth sometime in the afternoon, but had never looked at the clock, nor had her grandmother mentioned the time. Her heart was pounding with an adrenalin rush that made her feel unexpectedly weak. She stepped back, her right leg brushing the armchair behind her. Stumbling back into the chair, Ruthanne slumped onto the cushion and stared at the document. The father's name was Charles Wright, and the mother was Kay Stevenson. The names weren't familiar.

"Who is she?" Melody broke through Ruthanne's haze.

"Yes. Tell us her name," Elizabeth insisted.

"Here," Ruthanne said bending forward to hand the paper to Melody. "Her name is Audrey."

"Now I've already Googled Audrey Wright, and it looks like she resides in New York. Manhattan to be exact." Nan scooped up the remaining copies and stuffed them back into the envelope. All eyes turned to Ruthanne, who felt like a boulder was sitting on her chest. How could everything be that easy? She was ready to look through yearbooks again tomorrow at other schools. Swallowing hard, she forced a smile.

"What else did you find out about her?"

Nan was only too willing to share her research. She pulled out several folded papers from the pocket of the robe. Smoothing them out on the surface of the coffee table, they all crowded together to look at the information. Beth pulled an ottoman to the table and sat down, while Ruthanne knelt on the carpet. Audrey Wright was listed as the top-selling agent for the previous year, employed by the real estate firm of McMaster and Davis, Ltd. The youngest and most successful agent out of 20, she had garnered significant awards and was active in several charities, as was her family. The article prominently mentioned her father Charles Wright, the president of The Bank and Trust Company of New England, one of the oldest and most prestigious banking institutions of the last 150 years. Ruthanne gasped as she read, putting a hand over her mouth.

"Mama did good," Melody said. "How did she know these people? We sure never knew anybody who had real money."

"We don't know that Mama chose this family. The lawyer...Mr. Parker may have arranged it," Beth suggested, picking up one of the pages that included a picture of Audrey being presented with the Realtor of the Year award. "She certainly looks like you," she finished, handing the sheet to Ruthanne.

"This is surreal," Ruthanne said, gazing at the picture. "I'm not sure..."

"Not sure of what?" Melody asked.

"It's a whole lot to take in, Ruthanne. I know as sure as shootin'," Nan said. "We should probably leave you to your thoughts, while we all get packed for tomorrow mornin'." She winked with good humor at Beth and Melody, but there was a steeliness in her eyes that moved both women to their feet.

"I agree with Nan," Beth chimed in. "It's a lot to process. Mel and I will get some things packed for tomorrow."

"And I'll let Stephanie know we'll be gone for a few days," Nan added, rising from the loveseat.

Ruthanne sat in silence staring at the other pages of pictures—Audrey at a fundraiser for Special Olympics and running in the New York Marathon. There was no mention that she was married. There was another picture of her with her parents Charles and Kay, cutting the ribbon at the entrance of a new Boys and Girls Club. Her daughter was successful, attractive, and wanting for nothing. Why would she want to know her biological mother?

26

Elizabeth absently ran her finger over her cell phone, expecting it to ring at any moment. But there had been no calls since Tom's late last night. He would meet them in Manhattan to search for Corinne. He was angry, but it was different this time. She knew he was angrier with himself than their daughter. Heaven help Trevor if he'd hurt her or worse. She shuddered and stared out the window as they sped past the quaint B & Bs, salt marshes, and roadside stands with fried clams and corn on the cob.

The random conversation they'd tried to maintain fell silent as Nan focused on maneuvering through the heavy traffic coming off the Cape. I-95 surprisingly had light traffic. The road hummed hypnotically beneath the vehicle. Ruthanne rode shotgun today, and Melody slept against the door, her head cushioned on a bed pillow. She must have taken a pain pill with breakfast to be so out of it.

Elizabeth glanced at her watch. It was only 9:30. Tom had promised to be on the road by 6:00. He should be at the hotel by 2:30. Nan had gotten a special rate through one of her school's donors. It was outrageously cheap for a decent New York hotel. Nan was a bit of a mystery. Her connections seemed endless as she paved and sometimes ploughed a path to where they needed to go. How was it that Corinne's disappearance and the revelation about Audrey coincided? There were a lot of questions swimming in her head. Mostly she prayed, "Lord Jesus, help me find Corinne. Please don't let her be dead." Too many news stories about young women who disappeared ended badly. She refused to give room to the possibility, except she didn't know Trevor. Who knew what he was really like or capable of? Verses she'd memorized in high school to help her take tests flooded her mind. Fear wasn't an option anymore. It had already worn her to the bone, and she was sick of it. Verses from Philippians came back from Sunday School days.

Do not be anxious about anything, but in everything, by prayer and petition, with thanksgiving present your requests to God And the peace of God, which transcends all understanding, will guard your hearts and minds in Christ Jesus.

She'd been letting God know her requests for months. He'd been silent. How could she be thankful in this horrible nightmare that never seemed to end? But He'd allowed Ruthanne to talk with her and Rick and Leah to make contact. He had been watching over Corinne. There could be no other explanation. It certainly wasn't by chance. Her heart and especially her mind needed guarding at the moment. The tightness in her chest began to ease.

"Beth," Ruthanne said, turning toward the back seat. "Do you want to stop for coffee and a bathroom break in the next half hour?"

"I'm all right, but don't mind me. If you need to stop, go ahead. I'm fine." She looked at the silent phone in her hand again, willing it to ring.

Melody stirred, groaning softly as she adjusted the pillow against the window. Her eyes flickered awake. She stretched her complaining back while adjusting the pillow to prop her arm. The pain medication had worn off, and a dull throb pulsed under the cast. The traffic was picking up, and semis wove their way in and out of lanes aggressively. She saw Nan grip the wheel tightly as another truck pulled in front of them.

"We're going to find Corinne," Ruthanne assured Beth as she twisted around to look at her sister. "She's going to be all right."

"You can't know that," Beth answered. "I'm praying that you're right, but what if she's not OK? I couldn't bear it. I just can't." Her voice rose in agitation.

"Where are we?" Melody asked groggily.

"We've got a couple of hours yet," Ruthanne said.

"It might be a little longer," Nan announced. "There's an accident up ahead."

The SUV slowed with the flow of traffic that was trying to merge into one lane. A pickup truck and minivan were strewn across the median. The truck was on its side, along with crumpled bumpers and debris lying in the grass. The minivan's front end was crushed; the windshield shattered with smoke filtering from underneath.

"Oh, dear Lord," Nan cried. "That van is on fire. You can see the children in the back!"

Several cars and a semi had pulled to the left lane. Three men ran toward the crash. Melody roused herself, horrified at the scene unfolding in the grassy median.

"Stop. Stop, Nan. I've got to try and help them," she cried, tossing the pillow to the floor.

"Mel, you can't do anything. Your arm, remember?" Beth shot back.

"I can help them. Stop the car."

Nan managed to bully her way to the left-hand lane, stopping behind a black Escalade. Intermittent flames licked the undercarriage of the van as two men frantically yanked at the sliding doors. Another peered into the overturned truck, pounding on the window.

"I'll go with you, Mel. Come on," Ruthanne urged. She unbuckled the seatbelt and threw open the door.

"You can't, Ruthanne. You're not well...." Elizabeth clutched the headrest of the front seat. "I can't handle this. Blood...oh, I'm sorry I can't..."

Nan looked back at her and nodded. "I'm no good where there's blood myself. You would think that after raising three children and being a principal, I could. I cannot abide it. But I can pray, and so can you."

Melody sprinted ahead of Ruthanne, her sandaled feet squishing through wet grass. It must have rained in the early morning. The acrid smell of burnt wires and fuel saturated the air. The grass was gouged with trails of tire marks. She called out her credentials to the men. One had smashed through a side window with a shirt wrapped around his arm. Fumbling inside, he finally managed to wedge the bent door back enough to reach in. A toddler was strapped in a car seat, wailing. Her face and arms were flecked with superficial cuts. Two school-age children were strapped in on either side of the car seat, one with blood tricking from an ear and unconscious. The other whimpered, saucer-round eyes pleading. Smoke billowed from the rear of the van.

"Let me in there," Melody demanded. "I'm a nurse."

The man who'd pulled the door back made room for her to look at the children. He was built like a lumberjack, with a shock of red hair and curly beard to match.

She leaned in as far as she could to take the pulse of the unconscious boy. It was there, but weak and thready. "Do you have a knife? Does anybody have a knife?" she barked.

"I've got one," the man who was on the other side of the minivan pulled a Leatherman from his jeans. He had gray hair, cropped close to his head, and wore brown-framed glasses. He ran around to the other side.

"Cut these seatbelts and get them out. We don't have time to do this pretty. Who's in the front?" She slid back to allow the man room to work.

"Looks like the mother," the red-headed man yelled over the increasing snarl of the flames. "I don't think she made it."

"Get the kids and be careful with the little boy," she called over the racket of fire, honking traffic, and sirens. The gray-haired man slit the first seatbelt and scooped up the girl, who was no more than six or seven.

"She's in shock. Make sure they wrap her in a blanket," Melody instructed him as he handed the knife to the bearded man. The gray-haired man ran toward a small group of people near the parked cars. A couple of army blankets had been thrown on the ground along with a First Aid kit. The big man cut the belt that held the car seat and hoisted it to Ruthanne, who ran from the burning vehicle, Melody watched her sister hurry to the parked cars with the squalling child strapped securely in the carseat. An ambulance jostled onto the median, lights flashing.

There wasn't much time left. Melody's throat was raw from the smoke. She coughed painfully and looked through the driver's side window at the woman trapped inside. Although the airbag had deployed, the front seat was crushed against the dashboard. The brown-haired woman's eyes were wide and staring. Her neck lay at an impossible angle. Melody sucked in her breath and refocused on the big man struggling to find the last seatbelt. He barely fit through the opening and lay across the seat. Finally shredding it, he groaned and pulled the little boy from the van, losing his balance and falling flat on his back. He clutched the boy to his chest.

Melody heard herself yell for help and then felt hands pull her back. She saw two men grab the shoulders of the fallen man and drag him away as the van erupted into an inferno. The ground shuddered as the explosion lifted pieces of metal above the flames. They clattered and then thudded to the soft ground. She gasped for air, the pain in her arm arcing like electric shocks through her body.

27

The showerhead shot needle-like hot water over Melody. The water felt good, washing away the death she'd witnessed today. Her cast was wrapped in a plastic bag to keep it dry. Doing everything one-handed was a challenge and inconvenient, to say the least. Both drivers were dead. Eyewitness stories were conflicting, but all agreed the pickup truck driver was at fault.

She ran a hand through her soapy hair and then stood with her face upturned to the stinging water, letting it all rinse off. The little boy was critical with a head injury, but he would probably make it. The baby and the little girl had some deep bruising, maybe some internal injuries from the seatbelts that had saved their lives. She didn't want to think about the emotional bruising these children would suffer for years to come. Grabbing a thick towel from the rack, Melody stepped out of the tub and wrapped herself in it, tucking the end under an arm. The steamy mirror slowly revealed her face that still bore faint yellow traces of bruising on her right cheek. Everything else had faded away. She could still feel the pressure of the girl's small hand clutching hers as the EMTs loaded her into the ambulance.

"I want my Mom, please get my Mom," she'd wailed.

Melody closed her eyes, tears slipping through her lashes and down her face. She sat on the bed, anger welling inside at a God who would allow these little children to suffer, to take their mother. It wasn't right. It wasn't right at all. She could hear her father's booming voice preaching that the world was sinful and broken. It was because of sin bad things happened, not because of God. Had she ever believed that? If He loved people like the Bible said, why did He let them suffer so much? What had these children done to deserve this? She found a tissue and blew her nose.

She looked at the small clock by the lamp. It was almost 7:00. Everyone was going to dinner at an Italian restaurant down the street. After the trauma of the day, how could any of them eat? She found her cell phone at the bottom of her purse, along with the business card of the bearded man, whose name was Dale Mucher. He'd risked his life pulling the young boy from the van. He was a land surveyor who'd been on his way south for a vacation. She laid the card on the nightstand and punched in Beth's number. Her sister sounded disappointed, but said she understood. After finding a fluffy white robe on the back of the bathroom door, Melody wrapped herself in its warmth, curled up, and fell asleep on the bed.

The restaurant bustled with waiters hauling trays of pasta, and Dean Martin was belting out "That's Amore" in the background. The group followed the maître d' to a large corner table where Rick and Leah were already seated. Both rose to greet them. After quick introductions and handshakes, they concentrated on the menu. The orders were taken, and while Tony Bennett crooned "Fly Me to the Moon," the events of the last 24 hours were rehashed. Rick and Leah had been unable to locate Corinne or Trevor, but thought another conversation with some of the waitresses at the deli might prove useful. Tom agreed and said he and Beth would talk with them in the morning when it opened.

The landlord of the abysmal rented room was not to be found; a property management company was used. The company could offer no information as to a forwarding address. The room had been emptied of all personal items just a few dishes and a toaster remained. The rent had been current, a week-to-week arrangement.

Beth's stomach churned hearing the details of their daughter's bare existence. How could she be happy living like this? But more importantly, where was she now? With Trevor? Running from him? Dead in an alley or worse? She shivered and took a sip of ice water. Tom's face was lined with worry, not anger as she had expected. He put his hand over hers on the table.

"We'll find her. I'm sure the Lord will direct us in the right way," he declared.

Beth looked into his eyes, comforted by his confident gaze. Their salads and a breadbasket arrived. Conversation stalled while the waiter ground pepper and grated fresh parmesan over their bowls.

"So tell us about the accident on the way here," Leah said, turning to Ruthanne as the waiter retreated to the kitchen.

"It was awful," Nan said. "Melody and Ruthanne were certainly much braver than I was."

Ruthanne shook her head. "It was something we had to do. I just feel terrible for those poor little children." She recounted the rescue with a minimum of fuss. "Melody was an absolute champion in getting those babies out alive, as were those men. I just pray they'll be all right. I have the name of the hospital where they were taken. Maybe they'll give us an update on their conditions."

"I wouldn't hold my breath, you know, with all those privacy regulations," Rick said, spiking a fork into the crisp greens.

"Where is Melody?" Leah asked. "Is she all right?"

"I think everything crashed in on her when we arrived at the hotel," Beth said. "She really did put her life on the line today, standing by that van until the very last second. It was..." Beth stopped to control her emotions. She had been sure she'd see her sister die in front of her eyes today, maybe both of her sisters. Beth cleared her throat. "It was the most frightening thing I've ever seen. I don't know how either one of you stayed so calm."

"It's not what you think about when you're in the middle of it." Ruthanne smiled and pulled a piece of well-buttered garlic bread from the wicker basket.

"It was entirely amazin' to me," Nan drawled. "I am a devout coward in those situations." She looked over with admiration at her friend. "Have you told them your news?"

Ruthanne blanched, stopping mid-bite. Quickly swallowing, she said, "No. I hadn't gotten around to that."

28

"**I** am so sorry, darlin'. I had no idea you hadn't talked to the Longs about your daughter," Nan apologized. She pulled out a nightgown and robe from a red suitcase, shaking the wrinkles from both before laying them on the bed. Ruthanne and Nan were sharing a spacious two-bedroom suite.

Ruthanne grimaced. "It's not something I talked about with anyone from the mission. I guess I should have, but..."

"It's really no one's business unless you decide it is," Nan asserted. "I stuck my foot in it. The excitement bypassed my brain and headed straight to my mouth."

Ruthanne laughed ruefully. "Well, they know now. It's not a big deal, I guess. It was 30 years ago and before I had any connection with the mission."

"What would the mission do anyway?"

"I don't know. Nothing, I guess. I never felt the need to share that part of my life until now. Maybe that was wrong. I'm not sure." Ruthanne sat on the brown velvet sofa, sweeping her fingers across the plush fabric on the arm. "I'm going to check on Melody before I go to bed. Don't worry about tonight. It's fine. No offense taken."

She gave her friend a broad smile and a solid hug on the way out the door.

Tom and Beth spoke in low tones about the plan of action to find Corinne. Beth's head ached from the stress of the day, and Tom massaged her shoulders. She carried all of her tension in her shoulders, and he always found the right spots to release it. He kissed the back of her neck.

"Breakfast at the deli tomorrow then?" he whispered in her ear.

"Yes," she said.

"We will find her, Beth. Corinne is all right."

She lay back on the pillow; the soft cool sheets felt satiny against her skin. Tom leaned over and kissed her on the mouth. He left the bed and stood gazing at the glittering New York skyline from the large window. Beth watched his jaw work as if he were forming words. He finally turned to face her.

"I made some big mistakes in the way I handled Corinne and Trevor. I know that, and it's been hard to deal with—and to admit it. I really thought at the time she'd change her mind and see Trevor for what he is." Tom gave her a lopsided smile and shook his head. "I know you've been angry with me. I've been angry with myself and you. I feel like I'm walking on eggshells at home, and you've put up a wall that I can't pull down. I'm sorry for the way I handled the situation." He paused and then walked back to the bed. "We *will* find

Corinne. But I need to know that we're OK again. That we can get past this."

Beth's throat tightened as she struggled for the right words. "I love you," she said huskily.

Nan, Ruthanne, and Melody enjoyed a substantial breakfast in the large suite. Melody was finally looking more like her old self. Ruthanne commented that she had apples back in her cheeks, just like Grandma always said when she saw her granddaughters. Melody laughed and replied that it beat having a grapefruit in your cheek, which was what the bruises had felt like for a few days. With some makeup, the faint discoloration was invisible. She'd made an early call to the hospital where the children had been admitted to find that all were doing better. The baby might even go home later today. The little boy, whose name was Jeffrey, was awake and talking, and his sister was anxious to go home. The father, who'd been in Boston on business, had been located and was now with his children.

Melody felt a sense of relief, but didn't want to think about the horrible loss of a mother and wife. Life was all too short and unpredictable. It seemed unfair for her to sit here enjoying a hearty breakfast while these children would never have another meal with their mother. It was all senseless.

"You were spectacular out there yesterday," Nan commented to Melody, taking a bite of scrambled egg.

"It was something I had to do," she said, her attention returned to the conversation.

"Have you ever thought about emergency medicine or pediatric nursing?" Ruthanne asked.

"I did in the beginning, but I need more education. I really need my RN, not just the LPN."

"Girlfriend, y'all need to go back to school and get it then," Nan admonished. "You have a gift that you haven't even tapped into."

Melody studied her breakfast to avoid the eyes of her sister and Nan. She finally picked up a piece of bacon and bit off a chunk. "You're probably right, but with me, it's always the finances. I really don't want to take out loans, and I have to support myself."

"There're plenty of scholarships and grants out there. They're cryin' for nurses of all sorts. An experienced academic advisor would get you goin'."

Before she could reply, Ruthanne burst out laughing. "Guess who that might be?" she said, catching her breath. Melody noticed that Ruthanne pressed a hand against her side. She searched her older sister's eyes, who carefully ignored her.

"That fiery look in Nan's eyes is fair warning. Once the woman makes up her mind about a project, just stand back, because it's going to happen. You'd better be ready, Mel."

Nan sniffed, feigning offense. "Of course, I have experience in this sort of thing, and I'd be honored to help you get your career, well, where it should be."

Nan's brown eyes twinkled with humor and determination. "What do y'all have to say, Ms. Melody?"

Melody was speechless. This was the break she'd been wishing for her entire adult life. To finish her RN and work as a trauma or pediatric nurse was a long-lost dream. Dennis had never encouraged her to do anything except take as many shifts as she could so he could watch football in his underwear. Staring straight at the plump woman in the pink and purple silk robe, she nodded in agreement.

Tom and Beth sat drinking the deli's strong coffee while they watched the frenetic activity involved in serving an endless stream of people. They'd ordered eggs, bagels, and a sampler of cream cheeses. Beth had dressed carefully today in white linen capris and a silky blue camp shirt. She wore a small gold locket with a diamond in the center that held Corinne's picture, along with small diamond studs in her ears. The locket had been her mother's, and she'd promised to give it to Corinne someday when the time was right. She prayed that today was the right day.

Rick had told them to find a waitress named Lillian. She'd been a friend to Corinne. The nametag pinned on their waitress' white shirt said "Sara." When she came back with the coffeepot, they'd decided to ask if Lillian was working today. Sara, a strawberry blonde with an upturned nose and bright blue eyes, reappeared behind Beth, coffeepot in hand.

"Need a refill?" She asked, smiling. Her wispy hair was cut elfin-like around a petite face. She reminded Beth of Tinkerbell.

"Yes, yes, I do." Beth slid the cup across the gray Formica tabletop toward the waitress while Tom did the same.

"Do you know if Lillian is working today?" Tom asked casually as he reached for his cup. His gray hair was combed back from his broad, well-tanned forehead, now etched with lines. It was funny how wrinkles and the other stuff of aging just crept up on you, Beth thought. She hadn't noticed how prominent those worry lines had become. Tom wore a red golf shirt and khaki shorts, very casual clothing for her suit-and-tie husband. He poured cream into the coffee from a small brown pitcher.

"Uh, do you know her?" the waitress asked warily.

"Not really, but we'd like to talk to her."

"It's about our daughter, Corinne," Beth blurted out.

"Corinne? I don't think I know her."

"We think Lillian may. We'd just like to ask her. We're trying to get some money to her, and she must have moved recently," Tom said smoothly, sipping his coffee.

The waitress dropped her guard. "I'll see if Lill can come over. It's pretty tough with this crowd right now." Sara jabbed a thumb in the direction of a woman who stood with her back to them three tables away.

"Thank you. We appreciate it," Elizabeth smiled. "I think we should try some of those cinnamon pastries while we wait. Right, Tom?" Her husband looked up with instant agreement.

The wait for Lillian was long enough for the couple to almost finish the pastries and drink another cup of coffee.

Lillian was a short, sturdy woman with gray hair that curled like Annie's in the Broadway musical. She hurried over from the cash register after ringing up a table of eight.

"You're looking for Corinne?" Lillian asked, her jaws moving rhythmically with a generous wad of gum.

"Yes," Elizabeth began, struggling to keep her voice even. This woman must have children of her own. She'd understand the urgency.

"We're her parents, and we've been trying to locate her. I called here a couple of days ago and found out that she's not working here anymore.

"Yeah. That's right. I don't know what happened. Nice kid, Corinne. She's a sweet girl, but that boyfriend of hers is trouble."

Elizabeth saw Tom's face darken with anger, his jaw tightened. She quickly asked, "Do you happen to know where they might have moved to? They've disappeared from their apartment, or room, or whatever it is." She shuddered, remembering the cramped, dirty space.

"I really wouldn't know. Hey, could you show me some sort of identification? I'd feel a little better about talking to you."

"Sure." Tom sprang into action, his wallet pulled from the back pocket of his shorts with lightning speed.

Elizabeth dug into her purse to find her driver's license. Lillian looked at both licenses, satisfied that they were legitimate.

"OK, I'll tell you what I know, but wait until I get the orders for my last table. I'll be back."

Tom drummed his fingers on the tabletop as he watched Lillian slide plates of eggs and toast onto a table of elderly patrons. He and Beth locked eyes, both desperate to hear any word of encouragement.

"We'll have to go to the police if we can't find her today," Beth stated. They couldn't wait any longer. They needed help.

"I agree," Tom said. "But she's an adult, and I'm not sure they'll even listen to us."

"They have to. They're the police."

"This is New York City. Do you have any idea how many people *want* to disappear here?"

Elizabeth's heart dropped. He was right. Unless God showed them where she was, their daughter was lost in a vast urban wilderness. Lillian whooshed back to the table with a coffeepot in hand.

"I just have a couple of minutes, but here's what I know," she began. "Something was happening between her and that wannabe musician of hers. They were arguing in the backroom where we have our lockers. Corinne had been crying, but she wouldn't tell me what was going on, except she said, 'He can't make me do it. I won't let him.' She gave her notice that day, and I haven't seen her since."

"Did she ever give you a phone number, anything?" Tom asked.

"No. She always used the pay phone over there." She pointed to a beat-up black and silver phone on the wall near the bathrooms. "So she didn't have a cell or anything. Never saw her use one."

"What about other friends? Do you know if she hung out with anybody?"

Lillian shook her head. "No. The poor kid was always working, and then she had to get back home or the boyfriend would be mad. Wait a second." She pulled a pencil from behind her ear and tapped it on the table. "She mentioned to me that he'd started playing at a little club a few blocks from here. It's uh...oh...what's the name?" She tapped the pencil impatiently. "It's Diggers. No. Digby's. That's it. Digby's. A little club over on Scarlet Street. Go down three blocks and hang a right. It's on the corner. They might know something."

"Thank you," Elizabeth said gratefully. "We appreciate your help."

"No problem. I hope you find her. She's a good kid."

29

The yellow taxi wove in and out of the messy traffic in the direction of West 83rd Street. Once they turned onto the street, rows of expensive brownstones lined the sidewalks. Ruthanne and Nan sat in the backseat, watching nannies wheeling carriages and strollers toward Central Park. An orthodox Jew with long curls and black skullcap argued with another, who waved his arms about and kept walking. Businessmen wearing expensive suits and carrying briefcases hurried by.

She couldn't believe it was happening. An exploratory phone call would have been more to her liking; she'd even lobbied hard for it, but Nan would have none of it. They would make an exploratory visit, not a phone call. The taxi driver squeezed into an impossibly small parking space and looked back at the women.

"That'll be $25," he said with a heavy Middle Eastern accent. His head was wrapped in a white turban, his face covered with a dark beard. Nan fished the money from her bag, along with a hefty tip. She put the money inside a small gospel tract. His black eyes looked at her questioningly, but then he quickly snatched the cash, along with the pamphlet.

The heat rolled up in steamy waves from the sidewalk once their feet hit the concrete. An elegant black and brass sign identified the McMaster & Davis, Ltd. offices. Ruthanne felt sick. They couldn't just storm into this high-end real estate firm and announce that their top realtor was her biological daughter. She needed more time. They also needed a plan—anything other than this. Nan thrust her arm through her friend's and half-dragged her toward the brownstone's steps.

"Wait, Nan. Please, just wait. We can't just announce that Audrey Wright is my daughter and expect doors to open. I can't do this." Ruthanne extricated herself from Nan and nervously brushed back unruly gray bangs from her eyes, desperately wishing she'd brought some bottled water.

"I do have a plan," Nan replied. "You just need to be an innocent bystander...for now. Give me the portfolio. I think this may work, and you won't have to do a thing." Nan hiked her handbag onto her shoulder, squaring her shoulders.

Ruthanne pulled the black folder from a cavernous daisy-covered tote bag and handed it to Nan.

"What are you planning to do? You can't just spring this sort of thing on someone. I should have written, called something, anything."

"Stop worryin'. I am capable of being discreet, Sugar. Let's get out of this sun. It's absolutely uncivilized today."

They climbed the steps and entered through a forest green door that led from a posh foyer with a marble floor into a cool, sophisticated reception area. The carpet seemed to swallow their sandaled feet in its plum depths. Jazz played in the background. A tall African-American man with a headset wrapped around his ear and jaw welcomed them.

"Good afternoon, ladies. With whom do you have an appointment?" he quizzed and then glanced down at an open appointment book.

"Actually we don't have an appointment, and have but a miniscule window of time here in the City," Nan drawled confidently. "I was hopin' to speak with Ms. Wright. I'm Nannette Carrington Singletree, Headmistress of Blue River Academy in Nairobi. I'm sure y'all know my daddy, Senator Thaddeus Carrington of the great state of Georgia. I would truly appreciate a few minutes of Ms. Wright's time."

The man's discomfort was immediately obvious to Ruthanne, who could empathize with his dilemma in handling Nannette Carrington Singletree.

"Let me see if she's finished with her last appointment, Ms. Singletree. Won't you please have a seat, ladies?" he suggested returning to his professional demeanor. "May I get you an iced tea or perhaps an iced cappuccino?"

"Not for me," Ruthanne said as she sat on the end of a leather sectional that wound around the waiting area. She clasped her hands together to stop the shaking. She wished a prayer would come to mind. Her mind was a complete blank.

"I'd just adore an iced cappuccino," Nan cooed.

Ruthanne closed her eyes and shook her head in wonder at her friend's absolutely steady nerves. A silver tea service sat prominently on a small mahogany Queen Anne table next to them. Fine bone china cups in an array of floral patterns framed the service. They watched the man, whose nameplate indicated he was Marcus Watson, walk toward an elaborate coffee setup behind the desk. They could see he was speaking into the mouthpiece affixed to his face.

Nan smiled. "I'll bet you a bowl of biscuits and gravy that Miss Audrey Wright will appear within the next five minutes. Long enough to let me know I should call for an appointment, but not so long as to lose me as a potential client."

Ruthanne tried to smile back and noted the time on her wristwatch. Nan was incorrigible. She played the appropriate influential relative card to suit her purposes or the Southern belle card as circumstances warranted. For her to use the double whammy indicated how high the stakes were. In Nairobi, it was a different story. Nan had established her own reputation as an important businesswoman and educator. Blue River Academy, while educating the cream of the crop from embassies, politicians, and well-heeled ex-patriots, also ran programs for the very poor, from health education and parenting skills for women to basic reading, writing, and math for children.

"Three minutes to go," Nan reminded Ruthanne as she sipped the frothy, icy cappuccino. Ruthanne felt like a stone lay in her stomach. Three minutes to go, and she would see her daughter. She willed herself not to run.

The bus slowed as it pulled into the Rochester station. The air conditioning had died somewhere outside of Syracuse, and the last hour and a half had been stifling. The passengers were cranky and ready to get off... more than ready. The brakes hissed, and the driver finally opened the door. People hustled off, some to claim luggage from the compartment outside.

Corinne pulled away from the worn fabric seat, her T-shirt stuck to her back with perspiration. The cramping wasn't as bad, but was still there. No one had answered the house phone when she'd called at the stop in Albany. She should call her mother's cell. Maybe she should call Sonya or Paul. No. It was too awkward. Corinne bent to pull the small duffle bag from under the seat ahead of her. A wave of pain shot through her abdomen. She fumbled and unzipped the bag, searching for a bottle of aspirin. Finally finding it, she forced two tablets down without water. The bitterness of the pills stuck to her tongue. Maybe Kelley. She'd understand.

It was supposed to be simple. Nothing had been so far. The calling card Leah had given her still had plenty of minutes. She hurried through the milling crowd into the bus station. It smelled of stale sweat and old food.

Her stomach growled with hunger, but protested against the smells. Almost gagging, Corinne sighted a pay phone. Pulling the calling card from her shorts, she hurried to use it.

Tom and Elizabeth peered through the window of the darkened club. Digby's didn't open until four o'clock. It was two.

"Maybe we should go around to the back and see if someone is here," Elizabeth suggested.

"Maybe," Tom acknowledged. "But I'd rather check out the music store we passed on the way. Trevor's a musician. He may have bought something there."

Elizabeth reluctantly agreed. It was probably better than waiting around for another two hours. They were so helpless. The police had taken the report, but she knew it would be filed and not pursued. The couple strode briskly back a block to a dusty shop called Minstrel Music. Classic rock blared as they opened the door. A jam session was in progress, and the middle-aged couple stuck out like a sore thumb. Elizabeth ducked down an aisle, pretending to look at CDs. When she almost stepped on an unshaven young man sleeping with his back against the wall in the rear, she scrambled to rejoin her husband.

Tom smiled at his wife and strolled back toward the musicians. There were four of them—two guitarists, a bass player, and a drummer. One of the guitarists looked up in surprise. He stopped mid-strum, jerking his head toward a frizzy-haired teddy bear of a man who played bass. The music stopped abruptly.

"Hey, man. What can I do for you?" the teddy bear asked.

"Just looking for some help finding a guitarist," Tom began. "He plays over at Digby's. I think his name is Trevor."

The guitarists had muscular arms, Elizabeth noted uneasily. The taller of the two sported skull tattoos on each bicep, and the other had long, thin mousey-colored hair that hung below his shoulders. The drummer was young, very young with a ring in the center of his bottom lip and a tiny ring in his left eyebrow. The young men smirked, watching Elizabeth, who gripped her purse tightly.

"Trevor? What's he look like?" the teddy bear asked.

"Blond, maybe 5'9" or 5'10", medium build," Tom responded.

Elizabeth racked her brain for something unique to add. "He has a tattoo on his right hand. Maybe a knife of some kind?"

"Oh, I know who you mean. He goes by Aces Wild," the drummer piped up.

"Yeah, he's around. You gotta job for him or somethin'?" the stringy haired guitarist asked.

"I was hoping he was around to talk," said Tom.

"Haven't seen him today, but you never know," the teddy bear shrugged. "He comes in to jam sometimes."

"Mind if we wait around to see if he comes in?"

"Nope. Help yourself."

The music resumed with a crash of cymbals while Tom and Beth studied the selection of CDs.

Corinne sat on a metal bench outside the bus station. The fresh air had calmed her stomach. Kelley was just finishing work at an accounting firm where she was interning for the summer. She'd promised to be there within 20 minutes. Corinne tapped her foot against the pavement nervously. What was she going to do? Kelley just might tell her to disappear. She'd treated everyone badly, trying to prove she was an adult. She leaned forward, covering her face with her hands.

"Oh, Lord, what have I done? Can you ever forgive me? Can my parents forgive me?"

A McDonald's hamburger wrapper tumbled down the sidewalk and blew into her ankle. Bending to pick it up, she saw a woman with a toddler in tow hurry toward her.

"Sorry, my son dropped that," she said, offering to take the paper.

"No problem." Corinne handed the wrapper to her, eyeing the dark-haired boy in red shorts and white T-shirt. When she straightened up, the woman's face swirled away from her. Voices seemed to call to her, but the words were so far away, like being underwater.

Nan sat in a comfortable leather wingback chair in Audrey Wright's office. The young woman was tall, svelte, with piercing gray eyes. Her dark hair was shot with blond highlights, cut short to frame her finely boned face perfectly. Nan decided Audrey was a handsome woman, but not pretty, much like Ruthanne. The suit she wore was obviously expensive and tailored. The pencil skirt revealed long, athletic legs, attesting to her running. The French manicure was perfect, as was her makeup.

"Thank you for seein' me this afternoon. I do appreciate your kindness," Nan began.

"No problem, Ms. Singletree. What can I do for you?" Her dark eyebrows knit with curiosity at the black portfolio that lay across Nan's lap.

"I have some drawings that you might find of interest. They were done on Cape Cod quite a few years ago. The lady who drew them is now deceased, but the subject matter is of interest to her family, and you might be able to shed some light on them. Your family came up as a possible connection..."

"You have me at a disadvantage. I'm not sure how drawings might have anything to do with my family or with me. Are you sure you have the correct information?" The realtor toyed with her Smartphone, tapped the screen twice, and then looked back at Nan.

"If I could just show them to you, perhaps y'all might recognize the girl this lady drew."

Nan slid the two of the later drawings onto the glass surface of Audrey's desk. The young woman gasped in surprise. She snatched up the pictures to study them.

"Where did you say these came from?"

30

Nan sat back in the chair, studying Audrey's reaction to the drawings. She could see the slightest sign of fear in the gray eyes, and then she followed the woman's gaze to the wall on Nan's left. Audrey rose and carefully took down a black and gold framed drawing of two young girls on the beach. One was brunette, and the other was blond. Nan covered her mouth to stifle a gasp. It had to be one of Annaliese's drawings.

Audrey placed the framed drawing on the desk, comparing it with the others.

"I believe it's the same artist. Her name was Mrs. Carroll from what I remember."

"That's right. These were all drawn by Annaliese Carroll. Do you know why she drew you?"

A slight smile crossed the young woman's face.

"She was always there when we were at the beach in August. I got to know her over the years. She was always drawing and always by herself. She gave this one to me one summer. I was probably ten. It's of my sister and me. Such a nice lady. You said her family is wondering about these pictures?" Audrey sat down again and looked questioningly at Nan.

Nan hesitated before continuing. She didn't want to blow it now.

"Yes, they are. Mrs. Carroll had three daughters, and they vacationed at the Cape every August for many years. The last year they went as a family was in 1980 though. I imagine you weren't even born then."

"No. But close. I was born in May of the following year. I'm not sure what your point is. You'll have to excuse me, but my next appointment should arrive in a few minutes, so I'll have to cut this short, Ms. Singletree." She stacked the drawings carefully and handed them back.

Nan slipped them into the portfolio and stood, already acknowledging defeat. Without tipping her hand, she wasn't sure how to continue. What if the woman didn't know she was adopted or that she had made a huge mistake with the folded corners on the birth certificate?

"I'm sorry to take up your time. I know you must have a holy terror of a schedule."

"I do, but it's what I prefer," Audrey answered. She smoothed back a strand of dark hair, tucking it behind her ear. "I'll show you out."

Nan walked to the door, her hand on the knob. "You know, you bear a strong resemblance to Mrs. Carroll's oldest daughter. That quite piqued her interest in the drawings."

Audrey stopped mid-stride her eyes widened and then narrowed.

"What exactly are you implying?"

"Did Mrs. Carroll ever talk to you about her daughter Ruthanne?"

The fine features of Audrey's face crumpled. Her answer came in a whisper, "Yes." She turned away from the door, staring at the frame lying on the desk.

31

Tom and Beth stood in Digby's seedy bar. A sound tech was working through a maze of wires and amplifiers; another tech was setting up microphones. The stale smell of beer and cigarette smoke clung in the air, making Beth want to take a shower. The bartender looked expectantly at them, and Tom smiled.

"We'll have a couple of club sodas with lemon," he said.

"Sure. Coming up," the heavily mustached man answered, who must have been in his mid-forties. He wore a red bandanna around gray streaked hair. A leather vest over a bare chest and tight jeans completed the look. Beth guessed this must be a biker club of some sort.

They sat down on the stools, watching the band setup continue. Beth took a sip of the bubbly soda, while Tom squeezed the lemon wedge into his drink.

"Do you know if Aces Wild is playing tonight?" he asked, stirring the drink with the swizzle stick.

"Naw. He got fired about a week ago. The kid was trouble. The boss got a new band comin' in tonight. Black Lace and Arsenic. All girls. They're gonna be good," he smirked with a knowing wink.

Beth closed her eyes. "Oh Father," she prayed, "help us find Corinne."

She heard the insect buzzing sound of Tom's cell phone. Without missing a beat, he put it on the bar and glanced at Beth as he continued to make conversation with the bartender. She quickly snatched it and saw that the readout said Ben Howe. Why would the pastor be calling them? Slipping from the stool, Beth answered the phone near the bathrooms, away from the sound tech setup. Relief and fear wrapped itself into a nauseating lump in her stomach as she battled to keep her emotions in check while Ben described the situation. She told him they would leave immediately for Strong Memorial Hospital.

Ruthanne's cell phone sang out a couple of measures of Vivaldi's *Four Seasons*, yanking her back from her daydream of the beach. She hadn't dreamed about the girl on the beach in at least two weeks. What did that mean? Was her search coming to an end, or did it mean something else?

Beth's stressed voice greeted her ear, telling her that Corinne had been found, but was in a hospital in Rochester.

"How did she get to Rochester?"

"I'm not sure, but Corinne called Kelley Howe to pick her up at the bus station. When Kelley got there, she found out she'd been taken to Strong Memorial. We have no idea what's going on, but she's alive. I'm so grateful. The Howes should be getting to the hospital soon."

"God is good, Beth. I'm sure she'll be just fine. Have you and Tom left yet?"

"We're just heading out of the city now. The traffic is terrible, but once we get to the Thruway, I hope we can make better time."

"I'll be praying for her and you too." She noticed that Marcus looked up from the computer screen with a quizzical look. She smiled and refocused on the call.

"Thanks, Ruthanne. I'm so sorry to leave you in this search for your daughter. You'll be all right, won't you?"

"I'll be fine. Nan and I are heading back to the hotel soon. Should I let Melody know?"

"Please. I've tried calling her, but her phone goes right to voicemail."

"I'll track her down. Call me when you have news."

"I will."

The call ended, and Ruthanne slipped the phone back into her bag. She bowed her head, clutching the bag in her hands, begging God to help her niece and to give Beth and Tom traveling mercies. So much was happening all at once. It was nothing like she thought it would be. The vacation was crumbling, and she was exhausted. She could sleep for days and days.

The sound of Nan's voice from the hallway behind the reception area brought instant tension to her neck. She could feel the muscle knot and twist into her shoulder. Was this what she'd come for, or had they made a mistake? What had Nan found out?

Her full-figured friend walked out, looking as if she'd just bought the Empire State Building, the generously cut fuchsia and black flowered jacket billowing as she walked. Nan definitely had a satisfied look on her face when she said goodbye to Marcus, who stood and strode to the door to let them out to the street. Ruthanne felt as if all the air had left her lungs. Was it over? What had just happened? Nan hailed a taxi and practically pushed Ruthanne into the back seat.

"What happened, Nan? Why the hurry?"

"We don't have much time, girlfriend. You're going to meet your daughter at dinner tonight, and we need to get you fixed up."

32

Melody sat in the hotel's bar, waiting for Dale Mucher. She fingered the business card, still wondering if she'd done the right thing. At least both of her sisters were away from the hotel. They couldn't lecture her or give a withering look at her decision to meet a man she'd met at the scene of a horrific accident. She would have gone with Beth and Tom, but no invitation had been extended. Corinne was a smart girl. Beth was overreacting. What did she expect when they'd thrown their daughter out on her own? Maybe Corinne had taken off with the boyfriend again to really travel the world. And Ruthanne . . . she sure was acting strange about meeting her biological daughter. Watching Nan drive the bus on that meeting was something she could stay out of for now.

Then there was Nan's offer to figure out how she could go back to school and get the coveted RN. Trauma nursing—that was what she really wanted to do. Pediatrics was running a close second if that didn't work out. Her head was still spinning from the spontaneous opportunity.

And now she was going to meet Dale, who was from Albany, which meant he lived only a few hours away from Sheffield. She glanced at her watch and adjusted the injured arm's position on the bar. The cast was really making her itch today. Pulling her cell phone from the small shoulder bag, Melody saw the voicemail icon flash. She'd had the phone on vibrate and hadn't switched it back to a ringtone. It buzzed and she scanned the screen. Her attorney was calling. Maybe Dennis had signed all the divorce papers, finally. She punched the call button.

"Hello."

"Ms. Washburn?"

"Yes."

"This is Kyle Campbell. I wanted you to know that Mr. Washburn has skipped bail. Are you still in Cape Cod?"

Melody swallowed hard. What was Dennis thinking? Was he coming after her? "No. I'm in New York right now. Do you think he's after me?" Her heart thudded like a bass drum against her chest.

"I can't be sure. His attorney has an investigator looking for him. Of course, there is a warrant for his arrest. The police are doing their best. I wanted to warn you about this development."

"Thanks. I appreciate that. Maybe it's a good thing I'm not at the Cape. Will you call me if they catch up with him?"

"Of course. Ms. Washburn, please be careful."

"I will. Thanks." She pushed the end call button and took a sip of the Diet Coke in front of her. Just when she thought it all might come together for her, this had to happen. Dennis mucked up everything—again. The vastness of the big city was her one advantage. This trip was also under the radar, which was a bonus. Maybe she'd finish her vacation here and forget about going back to the Cape. Or maybe she'd stay here, period. The city had real excitement that Sheffield sorely lacked. She turned her phone off and tossed it back in the purse.

"Hey there, Melody." Dale Mucher entered the bar with a broad smile, his red beard curled tightly to his face. His brown eyes twinkled with good humor. Now that she saw him again, Melody liked the view. Everything had been such a blur at the accident. A strong jaw, thin straight nose, and his confident manner, all were very attractive. He wore jeans and a black T-shirt with "Bahamas" lettered across the chest, flanked by palm trees. An eagle tattoo encircled the bicep of his freckled right arm, a very well-developed bicep, she noted. They eased into a conversation about their favorite foods, and TV shows that made her feel like she'd known him forever. He was intelligent, loved his job, and seemed so kind. Dale was divorced, so he knew what she was going through. Dale ordered her another Diet Coke and a beer for himself.

Ruthanne discovered that Nan was not only her friend, but could double as a fairy godmother when they began the whirlwind shopping trip. She felt like Cinderella getting ready for the ball, and finally acquiesced to a new outfit—outrageously expensive in her book, but necessary in Nan's. It was an Evan Picone sheath dress with a matching jacket in periwinkle. She silently lamented the loss of the comfortable skirt and blouse that were now bundled in a box. Nan gave her only moments before they were back on the sidewalk to find the right pair of shoes. In between stores, Ruthanne finally managed to update Nan on Corinne and tried to call Melody again. Her phone went directly to voicemail. Sighing, she shoved the phone back in the bag. Shoes were found at last, low simple pumps that matched the suit perfectly. Ruthanne vetoed a trip to a salon.

"Really, Nan, I'm exhausted from all of this shopping. I need to rest before dinner. There's absolutely no time and no way I'm getting some fancy 'do.' I am who I am," she said firmly.

Nan smiled and leaned back against the taxi seat, closing her eyes. "Agreed. I have pushed you past reasonable limits. I am simply dog-tired anyway. I just don't have the shoppin' stamina I used to. Besides, you're perfect the way you are—as always."

Ruthanne chuckled. "Since you've finally slowed down, you can tell me how you managed this meeting so quickly."

Melody and Dale parted in the hotel lobby with assurances to each other that they'd meet again—soon. It had been a perfect evening, and Dale had been a perfect gentleman. He didn't get drunk; he'd pulled out her chair and seated her when they went to dinner. He'd made sure she was comfortable and had even cut her steak for her. It was like a dream.

She sighed and sank into one of the large overstuffed chairs near the fountain. Several couples were chatting, obviously waiting for someone else before they went to dinner. She could fit into a group like that with Dale. They would laugh, make clever jokes, and be the life of the party. Why had she been wasting her life away with Dennis? Dennis could go kick a brick. The ride up in the elevator gave Melody time to confirm her decision. If Nan wanted to help her find free schooling, it had better be in Albany. Dale was definitely interested in her well, at least she hoped so. There was only way to find out, and she'd wanted to move anyway. She'd have to get online and check out apartments in Albany. It was time she got on with her life.

The hallway was empty as she padded down to her room. She should see if Beth and Tom had found Corinne. Their room was two doors before hers. Knocking softly, she called out, "Beth. Tom. Are you back yet?"

The door swung open, answered by an elderly man, his long white hair arranged in a careful comb-over. He was dressed in tux, with a small white rose in his lapel. He obviously was planning a big night on the town.

"Who did you want?" he demanded.

"Uh...oh, I'm sorry. I must have the wrong room," Melody backed away from the door. How could she have made a mistake? The man slammed the door, and she checked the room number—4205. It was the right room.

What had happened to Tom and Beth? Realizing she'd turned off her phone, Melody dug into her purse to find it. The bag slipped off her shoulder and dumped onto the carpet. Cursing under her breath, she stooped to gather the wallet, makeup, and miscellany strewn in front of the opposite room. She felt like a one-armed crab grubbing around on the floor to collect the contents. At least she was by Ruthanne and Nan's room—unless they'd skipped town too. The door opened, and Melody straightened up to see her oldest sister dressed to the nines.

"Shazam, Ruthanne! Where the...heck did you get that outfit?

Ruthanne pulled Melody into the room and gave her the Reader's Digest version of the afternoon's events.

"So, Beth doesn't know what's going on with Corinne then? But she's in the hospital?"

"Right. She'll call, but I'm sure they're still on the road."

"And you're meeting your daughter tonight? Here? Wow! It's been quite the day!"

Nan laughed in agreement. "I think Ruthanne and Audrey need time by themselves. How about we have dinner together?"

"Sorry, but I've already had dinner," Melody grinned and batted her eyes. "With a man."

Nan and Ruthanne exchanged looks.

"It's not what you think," she declared. "It was with Dale—the guy who helped at the accident. He was a perfect gentleman. He's a great guy, in fact."

She shouldn't have said a word. They both looked like disapproving mothers. She'd been riding high on a heavenly evening, and now she felt like a flat tire. That thought brought her back to her attorney's phone call.

"Speaking of men, I got a phone call from my lawyer. Dennis skipped bail. So now I have to worry about him again. I hope the cops arrest his butt and soon." The thought of Dennis brought a new wave of anger; her face flushed with emotion.

"He has no idea we're in New York, does he?" Ruthanne asked.

"No. Absolutely not."

"That's good. I hope he's caught soon," Nan added. "Melody, I hate to eat alone. Why don't you keep me company at dinner?" she prodded. "We need to make a plan for your nursin' education."

Melody eagerly acquiesced. She had lots to discuss with Nan. "Oh, right. Sure. We do need to talk. I have some ideas I want to run past you."

"Good. Let's go to a little café I saw down the street. It's French, and the smells were wonderful when we walked past it on our shoppin' trip today." She turned to look at Ruthanne, who brushed her hair with short, quick strokes in front of the ornate framed mirror by the bathroom.

"The reservation is under your name, Ruthanne. Don't look like a deer caught in the headlights. You'll be fine."

"This is so exciting, Ruthie! It's just what you wanted, and now it's going to happen," Melody chimed in. "Plus, you look hot! You don't look like a missionary tonight."

Ruthanne gave her sister a friendly grimace. "Fashion hasn't ever been my forte."

Melody gave her a one-armed hug, holding the cast out like a broken wing. "You just have to tell us everything, and I mean everything afterwards. See? It's all working out for you."

Ruthanne sat at the small round table, draped with crisp white linen; a small battery-powered crystal lantern flickered weakly across the tabletop. A pianist, stationed at a grand piano several tables away, massaged the keyboard with "Clair de Lune" and "Moonlight Sonata." The atmosphere was relaxed, but her heart was pounding, her hands cold, and her stomach coiled like a snake ready to strike. Prayer had evaporated. She felt worse than when the doctor had diagnosed the cancer.

Ruthanne rose when she saw the willowy, impeccably dressed young woman make her way as the maître d' waved his hand with a little flourish indicating the correct table. Her eyes were definitely Danny's. They were a stormy gray, with flecks of blue. Her short brunette hair was highlighted attractively around her narrow face. Dark eyebrows arched as she stared at Ruthanne and then relaxed when Ruthanne extended a hand.

"Audrey?"

"Yes. And you're Ruthanne?"

"Yes. Please have a seat. Thank you for coming tonight. I know this must be an imposition and well...awkward."

Audrey took the offered seat. A waiter was instantly at her side, asking if he could bring her a drink.

"Pinot Grigio," she said turning to Ruthanne. "Do you want anything?"

"No. Water is fine for me."

Silence reigned while the women concentrated on the menu, and Audrey sipped the wine.

An appetizer of stuffed mushrooms arrived, along with a basket of steaming herb bread. The tightness in Ruthanne's chest began to subside. The Lord had handed this meeting to her just as easily as the tide lapped over the sand on the beach. It had been her prayer for months and even years to see her daughter. Now Audrey was in front of her, and the luxury of being tongue-tied was unaffordable. She must start the conversation, or the opportunity would be lost.

"It's hard for me to begin, but I must tell you first of all that seeing you is an answer to prayer."

"I can't say that I've ever prayed to meet you, but there's always been some curiosity about my biological mother."

"My friend Nan tells me that my mother gave you one of her beach drawings. It was of you and your sister?"

"Yes. She was a very kind lady. We saw her every August, sketching families and the water, lots of things.

I often admired her work, and sometimes she would give me a small drawing of a shell or a gull. The larger picture was a special gift though. My sister Pam and I had been fighting most of the day. She'd knocked down a sand castle I'd worked on for two days.

Ruthanne smiled. "Sounds familiar. I think my sisters and I had some similar days at the beach."

Audrey nodded. "Mrs. Carroll called us over and told us she needed our help for a picture. She had us start a castle all over again, with Pam actually helping. She gave each of us a drawing that day. She talked about you and your sisters too. How you were all grown up, but had made lots of castles on that beach. When I was older, probably around 15, she talked about you a lot. How you were teaching children in Africa and loved it there. She was very proud of you."

The conversation stopped as salads were put in front of them, and the cold, untouched appetizer was taken away.

"My mother was a very special lady. I'm proud to be her daughter. It's wonderful that you have good memories of...well, your grandmother. Your biological grandmother," she corrected herself. "It's a part of your story I never knew before. My mother was very good at keeping secrets from everyone." She hesitated, not sure how to continue.

"I know you want to explain why you gave me up for adoption, but here's my perspective. I'm not angry at you, nor do I regret being an adopted child. My parents are great. I've had the advantage of their wealth and connections. They love my sister and me. My career is skyrocketing, and my life is good. If the right man would come along, it would be perfect. But I'm willing to wait on that. My sister Pam hasn't done so well in that department. She's been through a messy divorce, has two children, and she's 28. I can appreciate your concern, but I assure you I'm well-adjusted and happy."

Audrey pushed the salad greens around the plate, avoiding Ruthanne's gaze.

"I'm glad to hear that your life has gone well, and you're happy. I would feel horrible if that wasn't the case." Ruthanne looked at her daughter again, seeing bits of herself, some of Danny, and even a reminder of her father. It was something in the way Audrey talked with her hands, a look, the way she ate her salad. "It's selfish on my part, but I'd like to tell you the story of your birth, if you're willing to hear it."

Audrey's eyes flickered with curiosity. "I am willing, but I have to be completely honest with you. I'm not necessarily looking for a relationship."

Ruthanne hoped her disappointment didn't show. It had always been a possibility that this meeting would be the only one.

"I understand," she said quietly. "It's OK. I will respect your decision either way." Every ounce of her being wanted to hold this young woman and tell her that if it had been possible, the adoption would never have taken place. She would have found a way to raise her. The now exposed guilt momentarily halted her words, but Ruthanne willed herself to begin.

Audrey smiled politely as Ruthanne began the story once more. It wasn't as painful as when she'd told her sisters. The emotions, the excitement, the romance—all of it poured out of her like a flash flood. She must tell her daughter that her biological father was charming, intelligent, and romantic. He'd swept her off her feet during that week of literary discussions, listening to music of all kinds, and passionate theological debates. Then there were the rainy walks on the beach, stuffing their faces with clam rolls and French fries, and visiting the art galleries. They'd barely noticed that anyone else existed. And then when he'd had to leave, their goodbye had gotten out of hand. When Ruthanne had returned to school in September, she knew something wasn't right.

"I was so sick and losing weight that at first I thought I'd eaten a really bad taco in the college dining hall." She smiled wryly and continued. "But when my period still didn't happen in October, I knew."

"Did you tell anyone?"

"No. I couldn't. My scholarship and reputation—it would all be worthless. Plus my father's church would probably have fired him. My mother asked me a couple of questions about my health when I came home for Christmas. By then I was gaining weight and blamed it on the 'freshman fifteen' hitting in my senior year."

"What about an abortion? Don't get me wrong. I'm glad you didn't, but they were legal at that point."

"Honestly, I thought about it for about five minutes, but I couldn't have ever gone through with an abortion.

Life is a magnificent gift from God. No one has the right to take that gift from anyone, especially not the mother."

Audrey smiled, quickly concentrating on her salad. Ruthanne took a sip of water before she continued.

"When I couldn't hide my condition anymore, I called my mother, praying that she'd be alone. Thank the Lord, she was. Mama made arrangements to come to the school right away. I was always surprised my father didn't come with her, but I think my youngest sister was a handful at that time, so he wouldn't have left her home without a parent there."

"You have two sisters, right?" Audrey left her fork on the salad plate and wiped her mouth with the white linen napkin.

"That's right, and I'm the oldest." Ruthanne took a bite of the Caesar salad, crunching a large crouton. The salad was probably delicious, but it was tasteless as paper on her tongue.

"I have one sister Pam, as I said. She's my parents' biological daughter. Pam was born two years after I was."

"Was that difficult for you?"

"No. Adoption has never been an issue. I have a good family."

Ruthanne thought she heard hackles rise in Audrey's voice. "I'm so glad. I really am."

"So what happened after your mother came to the school?"

"Emotionally, I was drained from trying to hide my pregnancy from everyone. My roommate must have known, but she never said a word. My mother took me to my grandmother's in Wellfleet, which is where I had you. Between my mother and grandmother, arrangements were made through Mr. Parker. My mother didn't let me hold you, unfortunately. Strict instructions were left with my grandmother. She was afraid I wouldn't go through with the adoption if I did."

"That must have been upsetting for you," Audrey sympathized. "Mrs. Carroll never struck me as such a tough cookie."

Ruthanne smiled. "As a pastor's wife, she had to be tough. I still don't understand how she kept it from my father. He was uncanny at finding out what his daughters were doing. I probably have to thank my sisters for distracting him, or maybe there was a church crisis."

"Did you finish college?" Audrey asked, watching the waiter take away the salad plate and replace it with her entrée of broiled salmon and asparagus.

"I did go back and finish. After I got my teaching degree, I spent some time in the public schools, but when I got my masters, I began exploring mission work. That eventually led me to Kenya and the Maasai."

"Interesting." Audrey picked at the fish, then sipped her wine. "I actually started my career in the New York City schools. I was really sure I could make a difference, but after a knife was held to my throat in the bathroom by a girl hopped up on cocaine...well, let's say I saw the light and made a career change."

Ruthanne's sharp intake of breath almost made her choke on the crunchy romaine. She took a quick drink of water. After a couple of swallows, she asked, "Were you hurt?"

"No. But I was terrified to go back into the classroom. It wasn't for me. So I went back to school and took some business and real estate courses. McMaster and Davis was looking for a new agent. I applied, and as they say, 'the rest is history.' I'm working on my MBA now. I should finish in December. Real estate has been very good for me and to me. I've found I can make more of difference writing a check, rather than being in the classroom." Audrey sat back in the chair with a satisfied smile.

"We are all gifted in different ways. I've never had the gift of making money, so I've stayed in the classroom," Ruthanne replied.

"I can admire that. There must be a lot of satisfaction in seeing those children learn to read and write. Things we take for granted."

"Very true. And I have the privilege of telling them about Jesus, who can make a real difference in their lives."

Audrey cleared her throat. "I'm sure that's...nice. My family hasn't ever been big on church or religion. We might go at Easter or Christmas. It's kind of a family tradition, I guess. "

Ruthanne smiled, thinking about her parents' conversations about the C and E families—the ones who only showed up at Christmas and Easter.

"I guess that would have been different if I hadn't been adopted." Audrey gave Ruthanne a wry smile.

"You're right, but I think you were meant to be part of the Wright family. I did a little research before we left the Cape and found that my grandfather and your grandfather Arthur Wright were friends many years ago. They were partners in a fishing boat at one time when they were young. Then Arthur went into banking, and Donald Erickson became a realtor."

Audrey's eyes widened with surprise. "Really?"

"Really. He owned Silver Dolphin Real Estate until it was sold after his death in the early 60s."

"That's a very successful real estate company," Audrey said appreciatively. "Too bad it was sold. You could have made a fortune if it was still in the family."

"True. But I'm where I'm supposed to be. I started out running away from my life in the States, but I found out it's the calling God gave me. The people in Kenya are so desperate for everything—education, food, healthcare, but especially spiritual things. The school that will open soon will help meet many of these needs."

"Isn't it primitive and dangerous there?"

"Sometimes," she replied. "But it's simple too."

The smell of cattle and fried bananas was suddenly as real as if she were sitting in her hut. Homesickness swept through her. She longed for the little children who clamored for attention and were so pleased when she picked them up. Ruthanne closed her eyes, seeing school-age girls, beads woven into their short braided hair. Young boys watching over the calves. Men herding cattle to new grazing. Mothers stirring pots of maize porridge with a baby sleeping in a sling tied over their shoulder. Clapping, dancing, singing, praying—all in joyous abandon during worship. When she explained what her hut was like and the daily routines for just cooking and washing, Audrey shuddered, squeezing her eyes shut.

"Too simple for me. No restaurants, clubs, or anything. Do you even have a car there?"

"No. I have a bicycle for longer trips. It's a hard life and very different from what most Americans know, but it's home for me and well worth whatever I've given up here. In fact, I don't feel I've given anything up—nothing of value that is, except for time with my family."

Audrey shook her head, puzzled. "Amazing. I admire your commitment, but I'd have to agree with you that I was supposed to be part of the Wright family. I'm certainly not prepared for perpetual camping."

"It's not for everyone." Ruthanne forced herself to laugh. "My sisters wonder about me too."

Audrey glanced at her watch. "I want to thank you for sharing your story, Ruthanne. I'm sorry to cut this short, but I really need to meet with a client tonight."

Disappointment lay in Ruthanne's stomach like the congealing sauce on the uneaten stuffed chicken breast presented artistically on the fancy gold-rimmed plate. "Certainly. I understand. Thank you for allowing me to share a meal with you. Maybe we can keep in touch."

"Yes. Maybe." Audrey stood and extended her hand. She shook Ruthanne's hand as if they'd just finished a business dinner.

Ruthanne sat motionless at the table, watching her daughter walk away, cell phone already held to her ear. Somehow she'd failed to communicate the most important thing to Audrey—Christ. It was on the tip of her tongue, but it hadn't seemed right. She placed the napkin on the table, rubbing the fabric between her fingers. This might have been her only chance. Audrey didn't seem interested in a relationship. Why should she? Her life was great by appearances. Suddenly, as if a voice whispered in her ear, Scripture came to soothe her disappointment.

It's not important who does the planting, or who does the watering. What's important is that God makes the seed grow.

33

Tom swung the car into the hospital parking lot, easily finding a spot on the first level of the parking garage. It was late—a little after ten o'clock. Ben, Tricia, and Kelley were still with Corinne. Ben had promised they wouldn't leave until Tom and Beth arrived.

They didn't speak as the elevator took them to the fifth floor. Beth gasped when she saw it was the OB/GYN floor. She saw Tom's face harden. She knew he was attempting to keep his tongue in check. She prayed that neither of them would lose their cool. Now was not the time for any guilt trips or "I told you so" remarks.

Ben met them outside Corinne's room. His face was weary. Reading glasses rested on the top of his head.

"Glad you're here safe and sound. What a long day this has been for you both." he commiserated.

"It sure has. How is she?" Tom asked.

"She's had a rough time of it, but Corinne is doing pretty well right now. She wants me to talk to you both before you come in. Let's step into the waiting room over here."

He motioned with a nod to a softly lit area with couches and recliners. Magazines were strewn across a kidney-shaped coffee table; more were in a wooden rack by a table outfitted with two coffeemakers.

"Have a seat."

"No thanks, Ben. We've been sitting for hours in the car. What does Corinne want you to tell us?" There was a definite edge to Tom's voice, and Beth took his hand. He squeezed it and then released her, going to the coffeemaker to pour a cup of dark liquid into an insulated paper cup.

"I can already guess what she's afraid to tell us," Beth started. "We are on the maternity floor."

Ben smiled sadly. "Corinne is pregnant, but the girl has been through literal hell in the last three days. Let me tell a little bit of what's been going on."

"I can imagine what's been happening. She's gotten herself into a mess, and now we're supposed to rescue her," snapped Tom.

"Tom! Stop it! Of course we're here to help her, we're her parents," Beth's voice rose, and she immediately remembered her own prayer just moments ago.

"Anger isn't going to help right now. She's in a precarious position with the baby. You both need to calm down," Ben admonished. "We've got some extra sandwiches in the room. I'll go get them. You both must be hungry. In the meantime, have a seat, relax, and then we'll talk."

Tom's rubbed his forehead irritably. "All right. You're right." He snatched the steaming cup of coffee and looked out of the window into the night. Speckled against the darkness were lights from buildings and streetlights.

Elizabeth heaved a sigh of relief and found a water fountain. The cool water slid down her parched throat, easing the gravelly feeling. Straightening up, she swiped off a dribble of water from her chin with a finger. Tom sipped at his coffee, still not speaking. She wasn't going to be the first to break the silence.

Ben returned with a white paper bag, a weary-looking Tricia following behind him. When she saw Elizabeth, Tricia hurried to give her friend a comforting hug. Elizabeth choked back a sob, wrestling with her emotions.

"She'll be all right, Beth. Corinne's just terrified that you won't want her to come home," Tricia whispered.

Elizabeth's heart felt like a lead weight. How could Corinne think they wouldn't let her come home? It was all Tom's fault. If only he'd kept his temper and hadn't been so awful. But that wasn't true. She was just as guilty as her husband. She'd let it all happen. Sitting down with Tricia, Ben opened the sack on the coffee table, pulling out two sub sandwiches wrapped in white parchment paper.

"Come on, Tom. Have a seat and let me fill you both in on what happened," Ben coaxed.

Elizabeth and Tom sat listening to their pastor relate their daughter's life over the last couple of weeks. It wasn't anything they wanted to hear, but it was necessary. Corinne had suspected she was pregnant and had gotten a pregnancy test at a free clinic, confirming her fears. The day she'd gone to the apartment to tell Trevor, she'd found him in bed with a girl she'd never seen before. There had been a fight, which ended with the new girlfriend deposited in the hallway. Trevor hadn't been pleased with Corinne's news and demanded that she get an abortion at the same free clinic. He was thinking of leaving with the new girl T.J., since she was a singer and played keyboards. They might make it big together. They had "chemistry," something that he now lacked with Corinne. She didn't understand him.

Elizabeth bowed her head, hands covering her face. If Corinne had only listened to them. She had known the young man was bad news. His cockiness and big talk reminded her of Dennis. She'd seen Corinne following Melody's mistake, running headlong into a bad relationship. Why couldn't women see through those types and stay away? She lifted her head to notice Tom staring out the darkened window.

Ben continued, perched on the arm of the chair, his tone matter-of-fact. Corinne had actually gone back to the clinic and had signed papers for the abortion to try and save the relationship. The schedule had been full for the day, and she made an appointment for the next afternoon. When she arrived back at the apartment, Trevor was gone with all of the money, except for what Corinne had squirreled away behind the crumbly drywall in a bathroom cabinet, which wasn't much. She'd decided to have the abortion and then go home. With no job and an unwanted pregnancy, options had run out. A nasty stomach flu hit her the next morning, accompanied by a fever. When her stomach had finally settled down, she'd decided to take a bus home. She couldn't go through with the abortion. The bus ticket had taken all of the remaining cash. By the time Corinne reached Rochester, she was dehydrated and quite ill.

"Is Corinne really all right then?" Beth looked at Tricia, praying the answer was what she wanted to hear.

"She's getting there. Corinne hasn't really taken care of herself. She's thin, Beth, and so sad." Tricia explained.

"And the baby?"

Tom looked at his wife, and then at Tricia. "Will she miscarry?" he demanded.

"She might. Corinne is about 13 weeks along."

"It would be a blessing if she did," Tom growled.

"Tom, this is your grandchild you're talking about," Ben shot back.

Tom stood and rubbed his hands through his hair. "I know. This whole thing makes me so sick. Corinne had everything going for her until all this."

Beth was silent, guilt bubbling up as she'd tacitly agreed with her husband's previous statement. Being a single mother changed everything. College was over...unless the baby was put up for adoption. Adoption had helped Ruthanne. It might be the answer, if Corinne didn't miscarry. But would she ever agree to it?

"Can we see her now? I just want to see Corinne," Beth pleaded.

"Sure," Tricia said. "She really shouldn't be upset right now though."

"Can you keep it together, Tom?" Ben questioned his friend somberly.

Tom thrust his hands in his pockets, shoulders hunched. He went back to the window and then turned around. Beth waited, holding her breath, afraid that he'd refuse. Finally he nodded in agreement.

34

The three women relaxed on the velvet sofas in the conversation area of the suite, sipping herbal tea. A small silver platter of tiny brownies dipped in fudge sauce and a bowl of large strawberries sat next to the china teapot. Nan had ordered celebratory room service, but the mood was decidedly gloomy.

"I can't believe she wouldn't want to get to know you. Especially after all this time," Melody protested. "What's her problem?"

"She didn't close the door completely, but I have a feeling she's very uncomfortable with having her life disrupted right now. I don't know her or all the circumstances. I'm just grateful that I got to meet her. It's what I asked for. And I am very grateful to God for that dinner with Audrey. He didn't let me down."

Melody huffed and took a bite from a large juicy strawberry. Ruthanne saw the skepticism on her sister's face. Mel wasn't off base. She wanted desperately to be content with what had happened, but she wasn't there yet. God had answered her prayers, but not exactly in the way she'd hoped. Maybe in time, she'd see the reasons a relationship hadn't happened with Audrey.

"I'd really like to hear what you two cooked up about Melody going back to school."

Melody's face brightened, and she launched into the ambitious plan she and Nan had outlined. She enjoyed watching Mel's positive attitude take over. Her eyes sparkled, and the pout disappeared from her face. Ruthanne hoped the unexpected joy in her little sister's life would take some of the sting out of the exhilarating and disappointing evening. Anger and guilt were at the door, banging away at her thoughts. The "if onlys" reared their ugly faces—if only I'd said...if only I'd begun searching for her sooner...if only I'd kept Audrey. A prayer for peace in her heart rose heavenward while Melody chattered.

"It sounds like a good plan. You do have an excellent advisor though," Ruthanne smiled at Nan. She hadn't heard half of the report, but with Nan at the helm, everything would be handled.

"Melody has a lot of work to do. First thing, she'll have a ton of paperwork that will make her mind go numb." Nan popped a petite fudgy brownie in her mouth.

"I'm ready for it. I'll make it work."

"I know you will. You're a Carroll after all. Remember what Daddy used to call us? His little gingersnaps. We were tough little cookies full of spice and everything nice." Ruthanne smiled at the memory.

Melody chuckled. "I'd forgotten about that. We *are* tough cookies."

Ruthanne slipped her shoes off and bent to rub her feet. She longed for bed, but she longed for Africa even more.

"So what do you want to do now?" Nan queried. She stretched out her pudgy legs draped with the silky flowered robe.

Ruthanne hesitated. She had a feeling from the look on Nan's face that she wasn't asking if she wanted another cup of tea. There was no point in continuing the Cape Cod vacation or pretending that she was happy in the States.

"I think this vacation is over. It's time for me to talk to the doctor about that other treatment and get back to Kenya. I want to go home."

35

few ragged leaves fluttered on the skeletal trees in the increasing winter wind. It was directly out of the north and decidedly blustery. Snow had begun falling, smothering the patchy colored grass of greens and browns. Melody shivered, pulled the wide coat collar up around her neck, and hurried to the house. It was her second winter in Albany, and life was good. Graduation from the RN program was in April— only four months away. Unlocking the front door, she stamped snowy boots on the mat and shed the heavy wool pea coat, hanging it on the coat tree by the door. Dude, Dale's ancient beagle, waddled from the kitchen and greeted her with a half-hearted bark. He was mostly blind and terribly overweight, but he seemed to manage despite his handicaps. The warmth of the house immediately thawed her icy hands and warmed her cheeks.

"Hey there, old dog," she said. "Did you keep all the bad guys away today?" She scratched behind his floppy ears, and the tri-colored dog groaned in satisfaction. Dennis had hated dogs and cats. They required care, which wasn't high on his list.

The quiet wedding ceremony almost a year ago was immediately after the divorce had been finalized. It had been the happiest day of her life. Dale was the real deal, and now that her graduation was so close, Beth couldn't criticize her life anymore. But she had to say that Beth wasn't as critical about a lot of things these days. Church attendance was still an issue for Beth though.

She and Dale didn't attend church, but they had gone to a Christmas Eve service at the big non-denominational church a few blocks away. Maybe they'd go again at Easter. Dale didn't seem to mind, and as Ruthanne had reminded her, she needed to be thankful for blessings received. She had to admit there were quite a few of those blessings in her life now. If things kept going so well, she might even consider going back to church.

The nursing program had been challenging and exhausting, but she'd excelled at emergency medicine. Dale had been a big encouragement. He'd cheered her on at every turn. She'd made friends at the hospital easily, and Nan had come through with complete funding for the RN program. There wasn't much to complain about, and she probably owed God some sort of church attendance.

Dale's grown children weren't so much of a blessing, but they tolerated each other well enough. Fortunately, his son and daughter lived in Pennsylvania near their mother, who had remarried years ago. The son was an auto mechanic, and his daughter was going to massage therapy school. Neither one was married.

Dennis had ended up in rehab for his drinking as a condition of his sentence for assaulting her. He'd also served some time in the county jail. She hadn't heard from him in months, which was fine by her. The last word on Dennis was that he had moved to Watertown, near the Canadian border, and was working construction again. With any luck, he'd stay there. He'd gotten religion, from what Tom and Beth had told her the last time she'd been to Sheffield. That must be something to see, she had scoffed. He'd only gone to church for weddings or funerals before. Imagining Dennis as a regular churchgoer was a stretch. It was probably all an act for his probation officer.

Melody changed from green scrubs into jeans and an ivory-colored fisherman knit sweater. Dale would be home soon, and she wanted to get some biscuits into the oven to go with the beef stew that simmered in the crockpot. Dude trailed after her, panting happily, his nails clicking on the hardwood floor. After shoving a pan of tube biscuits into the oven, she checked the email on the laptop which sat on the kitchen table.

Nothing from Beth today, but she was very busy. Her life had changed drastically over the last year. Melody smiled. Her straight-laced sister was a fireball of energy these days—passionate, outspoken, someone Melody had never seen before. It had to be mostly because of the beautiful new grandson, Keith. Beth talked nonstop about her daughter's courage to raise a baby by herself. But Melody had to admit Corinne deserved a lot of credit. She'd found a job and was taking online courses to finish school. She got her own apartment and hadn't asked Beth to be a fulltime babysitter. Now Beth had taken a lesson from her daughter and stepped way outside her comfort zone, working at a women's shelter. Maybe Dennis' conversion was the real thing, if Beth could change like she had.

She arrowed down through the junk emails until she saw the one from Nan. True to form, Nan had found the opportunity Melody was hoping for. It was available for the summer, although August was the best month to come. She'd already lined up a job with the trauma center at Brookside Hospital and told the staff there that she wanted to go overseas for a few weeks. There was plenty of time to work things out between graduation and summer. Nan had attached the application forms, and happily the organization was not religious. It was purely a medical organization. She pressed the print button, and the wireless connection to the printer window popped up, showing that the document was printing.

Before she could get to the printer in the den, the timer on the stove beeped that the biscuits were finished. The baking smells told her the timer was correct, and she pulled out the pan of golden brown biscuits. She hurried back to the computer to send an email to Beth. It looked like their summer plan would come together after all. The sound of a truck pulling into the driveway caught Dude's attention, and he shuffled off to greet Dale.

Beth put away the last of the freshly washed jeans in the plastic tub marked "Jeans, Size 14." Mindy, the other volunteer hung up a navy blue suit in the business clothing section of the small room that served as a used clothing boutique for the abused women who lived at Lilac House. The rambling Victorian was completely remodeled and had room for up to eight people at any one time. There were three women in residence with four children this week.

"Looks like we're finished," Mindy commented, straightening the clothes on the rack. She wore her brown hair pulled back, held in a large clip.

"I think you're right. I couldn't believe the donation from the Lutheran church today. There were tons of great stuff," Beth responded. "I know our church is sending toys and kids' clothing sometime this week. My Sunday School class has been collecting for awhile."

"That's good. It goes so fast here. When are you teaching the next cooking course? I might want to come to that myself," the young woman laughed.

Beth chuckled. "Next Thursday. We'll be making a chicken potpie and slow-cooker soup. I'm also going over how to shop for pantry basics and using coupons too. So many of these women just go to the drive-thru on the way home or pick up a pizza. I hope I can teach them that easy, yummy meals can be waiting at home for them. They just need a plan."

"Guilty," Mindy said, raising a hand like a student. "That's why I want to come. My cooking skills are pretty low."

"But your counseling skills are excellent. I've seen how Jackie and Maryanne are so much more confident. I'm sure they'll find jobs soon."

"I hope so. Their computer classes at the community college are almost finished, so we're working on their resumes right now."

"Good. Well, let's lock up. I need to get home and check on the chicken that's in my crockpot."

"I'm right behind you. See you next Thursday." Mindy grabbed her wool car coat from the hook on the wall and gave Beth a quick wave on the way through the door.

Beth checked the room, assuring herself that all was in order before turning out the light and locking the door. She pulled out of the small parking area at the back of the house. Christi, one of the new residents, walked up the front steps as she turned down the street. A year ago, being a part of this ministry would have been out of the question. Watching her daughter struggle to overcome Trevor's emotional abuse and so many obstacles in being a single mother had prompted her to step out of the safety of the church walls to Lilac House. Corinne had come such a long way in a short amount of time. She'd become a wonderful mother, and was finishing college at the same time. She'd taken on all responsibilities without complaint, surprising even her brother.

The women at Lilac House were escaping sometimes many years of abuse, both emotional and physical. Their children were scarred with fear and uncertainty, which was manifested in behavioral problems. When Tricia Howe had first mentioned the serving there, she'd scoffed at the idea mostly out of sheer terror. She'd always been busy with service within the church—missions, youth, and teaching. She felt her skills were meager offerings compared to the needs of abused women and children. She'd been a homemaker for all of her adult life, and she was the one who'd always helped her mother in the kitchen, in the church nursery, or had been in a Sunday School class. Keeping her home comfortable and orderly, taking care of her family, was what she loved.

Sometimes Beth felt that she should have gone back to college or done something grander with her life, but the training at Lilac House and encouragement from the other volunteers made it clear her skills were needed by the women who came there for refuge. She'd also had the privilege of praying with Karen, who'd received Christ after a Bible study. The thirty-something mother of two girls had escaped the constant physical abuse from her husband six months ago. He'd been arrested and was now serving two years in prison. Karen had begun attending her Sunday School class, and the women at church had shown love and concern right away. Slowly, but surely, Karen and her daughters were making progress and putting their lives back together.

Beth turned onto Sunnyside feeling a real sense of peace. God was teaching her about balance—church, home, ministry. Things with Tom were much better too. He had been supportive when she'd made the decision to take the volunteer training. He'd even started going to the jail to help the chaplain counsel the inmates. His focus was much less on more hours at the office too. They were both finding balance.

The most astounding ministry that had arrived at their very door was Dennis. He'd come to them searching for direction and asking for their forgiveness. Tom had counseled him for several months, and then one evening Dennis received Christ as his Savior. The incredible change in her ex-brother-in-law's life had been a wonder to watch. He hungrily studied the Bible, came to church with them, and joined a men's Bible study. When the job opportunity in Watertown had come awhile ago, he'd been sure God's hand was leading him to a better life. Dennis still called Tom regularly and kept him updated on his job and the small church he attended. If only Melody could see the transformation. It might encourage her to find the road to faith again. If only Daddy could have seen the change. She wondered what their father would have said about it. Mama would have killed the fatted calf in celebration. At least Dale was a good man, and Melody seemed happy for the first time in a long while.

The garage door closed behind as she turned the ignition off. Now the next adventure would be in Africa. Serving with Ruthanne would be the adventure of a lifetime. Her passport had come in the mail just two days ago, and the confirmation of her eligibility to serve in Maasai land had been yesterday's email. Regular correspondence with Ruthanne was a joy. The school in

Kenya was going well, and the church was growing. She was anxious for her sisters to join her so they could experience Africa. If Melody could find a way to get there, the three of them could continue the vacation they'd abandoned almost two years ago. It wouldn't be a leisurely vacation, but it would be one they'd never forget.

36

Corrine buckled the toddler into the car seat. The snowsuit made it difficult. It was like squishing a marshmallow under the tight straps. She'd be glad when winter was over.

"There, little man," she said snapping in the last buckle. "We'll go home now."

The dark-haired boy with rosy cheeks and brown eyes squirmed in the seat, grunting against the harness.

"Have a cracker, Keithy," she said, quickly finding a plastic bag of graham crackers in the oversized diaper bag on her shoulder. The boy's eyes lit up, his thick lashes framing wide-set eyes.

"Ca-ca," he crowed, snatching the brown cracker from his mother's hand.

Corinne slid into the driver's seat and looked back at the contented little boy. He was happy for the moment. She could only hope he'd stay that way for the 10 minutes it took drive to their apartment from the daycare center. Then the evening routine of dinner, bath, and story time would drain the rest of the early evening away. Fatigue swept over her just thinking about it.

It was worth it. Entirely worth it. Keith was a miracle all by himself. It would be nice to have another person to help at night though. Her job as a secretary at the law firm was demanding, and the online courses she was taking to complete her business degree took the rest of her time. The end was in sight. By May or June, all the requirements should be met for the degree program. The law firm was even paying for these last two courses.

She turned the wipers on against the thickening flurries. It might really storm tonight; the wind was starting to blow the light snow around like whorls of brilliant luminescent cotton.

The apartment house was on the other side of Sheffield. It was far enough from her parents, but close enough too. Things were good with them again. They loved Keith and spoiled him rotten but sometimes though, her father seemed distant. She thought she could see disappointment in his eyes when he looked at her. Could she ever make him proud of her again? Maybe finishing her degree would help.

Pulling into the driveway, she took the last spot next to the Riley's old minivan. The couple had three kids— two boys and a girl. They were a nice family. Heather Riley had helped her with Keith when he had caught a bad cold. She'd produced a vaporizer and Vicks to help his croupy cough.

She unbuckled Keith and balancing him on her hip, slipped the diaper bag strap onto her other shoulder.

She hoped the steps into the rambling apartment house weren't icy.

"Need some help?" a male voice asked from the darkness.

Corinne took a step back, dropping the diaper bag into the snow that was already halfway to her knees.

"Trevor! What do you want?" she demanded. Her heart pounded in her ears.

Trevor emerged from the line of vehicles and picked up the diaper bag. He was dressed in a ski jacket and dark knit cap. A shabby goatee gave his face an unkempt look. Even though he wasn't a big man, his stance was menacing. She felt his eyes linger on her with that longing she'd once found exciting. Now it just made her skin crawl.

He took a step toward her. "I thought I'd see my son."

"You should have called first. This isn't a good time."

Trevor stepped still closer. He extended a hand as if to touch Keith's cheek. The toddler giggled and waved. Corinne backed away, her arms tightly wrapped around her son.

"He's a smart boy. Knows his father."

"Wishful thinking, Trev. He has no idea who his father is, and it's going to stay that way."

His eyes glittered malevolently. "I have rights. I can get visitation or even custody. I'd watch my step if I were you."

This was the scene she'd feared ever since Keith was born. She knew sooner or later Trevor would come sniffing around to cause trouble. He hadn't been interested in fatherhood when she'd left New York. She'd kept a low profile since coming back home, but it was too easy to find people. He'd probably Googled her name and located her in seconds.

Keith began to squirm in her tight grip. The toddler complained with grunting and a half-cry. She felt him begin to slide. Hoisting him back to her hip, she turned toward the steps illuminated in the snow by bright porch lights.

"Just a minute, Keithy. Mommy's going inside in just a minute."

"The mommy gig suits you. You're looking very hot. I'll help you with him. He looks pretty heavy." He dropped the diaper bag in the snow and reached to take Keith.

"No! Please go, Trevor." She tried to keep the fear out of her voice. Keith began to complain again. He wiggled, twisting against his mother's grasp. "I need to get the baby inside. You need to go."

The front entrance opened wide as the Riley family tumbled out into the parking lot. The two boys ran ahead, picking up handfuls of snow and whipping them at each other.

"Hey! A.J. and Brayden! Cut it out now," Brian Riley called out. "Ms. Corinne is out here with the baby."

The boys dropped their snowball ammunition and trotted to the minivan, pushing each other, obviously hoping for a fall.

"Sorry about that, Corinne," Brian apologized.

"No problem. They're just having fun," Corinne said with relief as she watched Heather come down the steps with her daughter Katy trailing behind.

Trevor shifted uneasily, easing away from Corinne as the family trooped down the sidewalk. He pulled the knit cap down further over his forehead.

"Hi, Corinne," Heather said brightly as she glanced at Trevor. "We're headed to McDonald's tonight. Want to join us? Brian can put the car seat in the van for you." Her eyes followed Trevor as he sidled outside the pool of light. "Unless you've got other plans."

Corinne exhaled slowly with relief and adjusted Keith, who twisted and slid from her hip into the snow.

"No. I don't have any plans. Sure, we'd love to go. I don't feel like cooking anyway."

Heather called to Brian to come back to get Corinne's keys. Then she scooped up Keith, while she and Corinne walked out to the parking lot. Brian looked questioningly at his wife as he took the keys. She smiled and turned slightly toward Trevor, who melted into the snow-blown night.

The warmth and the hum of activity at McDonald's gave a sense of safety to Corinne as she pulled off Keith's snowsuit and settled him into a highchair. She slid the chair toward the large booth where the Rileys had crammed themselves, making room for her and Keith. She collected the excess trays and deposited them by the condiment station. Corinne bit into the large burger, while Keith munched happily on French fries.

"Was that guy giving you some trouble?" Brian asked, unwrapping his double cheeseburger.

"You might say that. He's Keith's father."

"You're kidding! He had the nerve to show up now after all this time?" Heather exclaimed.

"I knew it would happen at some point," Corinne sighed. "He scares me though. I don't trust him at all, especially the way he looked tonight."

"You might want to stay with your family," Brian advised.

"That's a good idea, Corinne. I get a bad feeling from that guy," Heather agreed.

"I don't want him running me out of my home. It's not right."

"No. It's not, but you have Keith to think about," Brian said grimly. "You might need to contact the police too."

"What's the custody arrangement?" Heather asked.

"He has none. He took off months before Keith was born. I got an order from the Family Court that he had abandoned Keith. I had no idea where he was."

"He can always dispute it and get visitation rights," Heather chewed thoughtfully on a fry. "You should talk to the family law attorney at your firm."

"I should. I can't bear to think of Trevor actually taking Keith. He might try to take him for good." She shuddered at the possibility.

"Why don't you give your parents a call? I'd feel a lot better if we could drop you off there tonight." Heather took a sip of steaming coffee, placing her free hand firmly on A.J.'s arm, cocked to shoot a fry at his sister. Brayden grinned and flicked one with his fingers across the tabletop. He got "the look" from his father, which ended the contest. Katy sniffed at her brothers and ate another chicken nugget she had drowned in barbeque sauce.

"You're right. I can't take any chances—at least not tonight." She pulled her cell phone from the diaper bag and made the call. She noticed a Jeep Wrangler with a hunched, silhouetted figure in the driver's seat parked near the exit as Brian carefully drove the minivan out into the swirling flakes.

The warm, comforting smells of her parents' house greeted them as her father took Keith from her arms. Her mother had been baking. Cinnamon and apple fragrance wafted from the kitchen. It had to be either apple cake or apple pie. There was a crackling fire in the brick fireplace in the living room. The couch was cluttered with an afghan, newspapers, an old Bible, and a crossword puzzle magazine. Dessert plates with the remains of apple pie sat on the coffee table. Corinne giggled silently. It suddenly occurred to her that her parents' living room reminded her of Grandpa and Grandma Carroll's. Grandma Carroll always had something baked, and Grandpa had his Bible and the newspapers strewn over the coffee table. He read constantly and was ready to share the information gleaned without provocation. Now her mother, who'd always been so particular about the house, was much more relaxed these days about housekeeping. Maybe it was her age or she was just getting more like Grandma Carroll. Were daughters always destined to become their mothers?

Grandpa and Grandma Carroll had spent a lot of time with Corinne and her brother—gardening, making paper dolls, woodcraft projects in the barn, rescuing baby birds that had fallen from their nest. Her parents were doing the same things with their grandchildren. The twins and Matt loved being here. The family Sunday dinners were relaxed and happy. It was good to be home.

Memories of her paternal grandparents sprang up that were a total contrast. They lived in Florida, visiting only during the summers to escape the oppressive humidity of St. Petersburg. They'd always seemed trendy and energetic, but distant. They were busy with their lives, which mostly included shuffleboard, golf, and cruises. Her grandmother had died right after she'd graduated from high school. Grandpa Hartman now spent all his time in Florida and didn't care to travel anymore.

Sinking onto the cushions of the couch, Corinne felt like a baby bird who'd taken a big fall from the nest, and now she had her own nest and baby to think about.

"Are you all right, Corinne?" Elizabeth asked her daughter.

"I'm OK, Mom," she sighed leaning back against the corduroy cushions, willing the knot in her neck to dissipate as she rubbed it with cold fingers. "I knew he'd show up someday, but I really didn't need that to happen tonight."

"It's terrible out there," Tom announced as he vainly attempted to unzip the snowsuit from his squirming grandson. "Hold on there, big Keith. Beth, can you get him out of this?" He handed the bulky toddler to his waiting grandmother.

"Men!" she playfully exclaimed, unzipping the suit in one smooth motion. "All right, there you go. Now go see Grandpa."

Keith squealed and ran slightly off balance to Tom, who hoisted him up and then swung him overhead.

"What are you going to do?" Elizabeth asked, sitting down next to Corinne. She stacked the newspapers on the coffee table to make room.

"I guess I should talk to a lawyer. Trevor may try something."

Tom brought a bucket of wooden blocks into the living room and settled Keith down in front of them. "He *will* try something. You need to inform the police he's in town. There's no way you can trust him for a minute around this little guy."

"I hate to do that. But you're probably right. I can't take a chance. He really scares me, Dad." Her voice cracked as she fought back tears.

"With good reason. He's no..."

"Tom. We all know. This is about what we're going to do now." Elizabeth's voice was firm.

Corinne smiled gratefully at her mother.

"Right," he relented. "Do you need anything from the apartment tonight? I'll take you over there. You can get your car before it's buried under two feet of snow. It's really beginning to storm."

"I do need to pick up a few things. We'd better get going though. Keith needs a bath, and it's past his bedtime. She glanced at the antique clock over the mantle. It was 8:15 already.

"I'll give Keith his bath. I have some extra diapers and pajamas here. You go with your Dad before it's a blizzard."

Corinne climbed into the passenger seat as her father opened the garage door. He backed the SUV into the driveway, pushing through the deep snow. There had to be at least 12 inches already. He engaged the four-wheel drive and headed for the Washington Street Apartments. The heater and defroster were blowing cold air. She rubbed her gloved hands together, watching their foggy breath twirl near the windshield.

"It'll be warm in a minute," her father assured her.

Lights from behind them glared into the vehicle. The driver dimmed the headlights almost immediately. She looked back and saw that it was a Wrangler. Hadn't she seen that vehicle at McDonald's?

The storm was making it almost impossible to see. The wipers thudded rhythmically against the onslaught of white.

"Do you know what Trevor was driving?" Her father glanced in the rearview mirror.

"No. It was dark and snowing by the time I got home."

"Does he drive a Wrangler?"

"He had a little car when we were in New York, but I think I saw that Jeep at McDonald's tonight. Do you think he's following us?"

"I'm not sure, but call your mother and tell her to make sure everything is locked up."

She dug the phone from her coat pocket and hit "2" on the speed dial. There was no answer.

"She's probably got Keith in the tub and can't get to the phone," she said, turning again to watch the headlights trail off to a judicious distance. A snowplow slogged its way through the street ahead of them, the snow spray spattering the windshield. "If he's following us, then they should be all right, don't you think?" she asked anxiously.

"*If* he keeps following us," her father answered. "If he turns around..."

"Maybe we should go back then, just to make sure." Corinne shivered, her gloved fingers interlaced and pressed against her stomach.

"Keep an eye on the vehicle. I have to turn at this light. If he doesn't follow, I'll turn around."

Tom slowed the SUV and made the left turn as the light turned green. The tires locked suddenly, sliding on a patch of black ice under the hard packed snow. He let up on the gas, narrowly avoiding a stopped snow-covered car with four-way flashers blinking in the driving lane. Tom brought the big vehicle to a stop. Corinne gripped the dashboard, her heart pounding.

"I don't see the Wrangler," she gasped, twisting around in the seat.

"I'm turning around in this driveway and going back to the house. I want to make sure your mother and Keith are all right."

Tom quickly backed out into the street to retrace their trek. The Wrangler was nowhere in sight. A couple of pickups and a few cars crawled along as the SUV churned through the snowy streets, but traffic was sparse. The wind died down, allowing them to get a good view of any vehicles on the street or in driveways once they turned onto Sunnyside.

"There it is!" he exclaimed.

The Wrangler was across the street from the house, partially submerged in a snowdrift. Drifts were piling up on each side of the street. The snowplow still hadn't made a sweep down Sunnyside yet. Before Tom could bring the SUV to a complete stop in the driveway, Corinne opened the door, stumbling into the snow toward the front door. The door was locked. Her father was beside her in an instant with his key.

"Beth, where are you?" he demanded as he stepped through the doorway.

"What's going on?" Elizabeth asked, coming from the kitchen, wiping her hands on a towel. Keith ran past her, lifting his arms up to his mother, freshly bathed and dressed in a heavy blanket sleeper.

"Keithy, you're all right," Corinne said with relief, hefting the boy with damp dark curls into her arms. He clung to her neck giggling, "Mama home. Mama home."

Tom's eyes were dark and angry, his jaw set. "Lock the door behind me. I'm going to check out that Jeep."

Corinne quickly explained to her mother what they thought Trevor was up to.

"Oh, no! The back door is unlocked." She scrambled to the back entryway. Corinne could hear the lock click into place. "Should I call the police?" her mother asked.

Corinne peered out the front windows, hiding herself behind the heavy drapes. Keith had gone back to the coffee table to pull newspapers apart, tearing them. Beth shook her head at the little boy and snatched the newspapers away.

"I don't know, Mom. We're not even sure it's Trevor."

She watched her father knock on the window of the Jeep. The window went down. The streetlight illumined the driver's side well enough to see that Trevor was the driver. Her stomach was roiling.

"It's him. Oh, Dad, be careful!"

"What's happening?" Beth pulled back the drapes to get a better view.

Tom was obviously telling Trevor off; he waved his hands and then stood with arms folded across his chest. The window was rolled up, and Tom backed away from the vehicle. He turned to hurry back to the driveway and up the sidewalk. They watched the Wrangler pull away slowly and disappear into the storm. Elizabeth slid the lock back and opened the door for her husband.

"Are you all right?"

Tom stomped his boots on the large mat and took off his ski cap. He tossed the heavy suede leather coat on the Deacon's bench along with the hat.

"I'm fine. Just fine," he said, forcing a smile.

"What happened then?" Elizabeth insisted.

"It's all right," he said, hugging her. "Let's sit down, and I'll tell you."

Keith struggled to climb into his grandfather's lap, a chubby fleecy leg pushing off the edge of the cherry coffee table. Tom hauled the boy onto his lap. Keith immediately snuggled into the crook of his arm, thumb firmly plugged into his mouth.

"I reminded Trevor that if he wanted contact with his son, there were certain obligations, financial as well as family obligations that would have to be met. After the way he treated Corinne and abandoned her and his son, he doesn't have any rights. He gave them up when he told her to get an abortion. I also told him the police will become involved if he comes anywhere near Corinne or Keith again." Tom paused and lowered his voice. "He's a coward, and I don't think he'll be back."

Her mother patted his shoulder. She gently extricated Keith from his grandfather's arms and started up the stairs. Keith wrapped his arms around her neck, his face already flushed with sleep. His eyes opened for second and then closed.

"I hope so, Dad," Corinne said, walking back to the front windows. She stood watching the snow deepen, the blackness of the night almost erased by white. She knew he was out there, waiting for them, no matter what her father said.

37

Corinne pulled up to the daycare center, carefully assessing the parked cars. No Jeep was in sight. She would talk with one of the attorneys today and get some sort of restraining order on Trevor. He could be charming and very convincing. How well she knew that. Pulling Keith from the carseat, she made a mental list of whom she'd need to talk to at the center before leaving today.

Keith, warmly clad in a light blue snowsuit, waddled up the sidewalk beside his mother, his mittened hand firmly held in hers. Adrene Starling, one of the workers, opened the door and greeted the pair. She was short and plump with rosy cheeks, auburn hair arranged in a smooth pageboy. She was dressed in black pants and a heavy pink turtleneck sweater.

She smiled, bending to greet Keith. "Good morning, big boy."

He smiled and patted her face with his free hand.

"Hi," he said and plopped himself on the snowy, wet floor. Mothers pulling at their toddlers and herding them to the playroom gave her impatient looks.

"Oh, Keithy, come on. You can't take off your suit here." Corinne pulled the toddler back onto his feet. He went limp in protest, dangling from her hand, erupting in a wail. She caught sight of the wall clock as she stood up. "Oh, great. I'm going to be late. Keithy, don't start this. I've got to…"

"Here, Keith. Come with me," Adrene coaxed. "We've got crackers in our room. Let Mommy go to work and we'll have a good time with the trucks and tractors today."

Keith snuffled, and tears dripped from his cheeks as he took the woman's hand. Corinne sighed and blew a kiss to the retreating form of her son. She'd call the director after she got to work to explain the Trevor situation.

Hurriedly parking her car behind the large, two-story Georgian-style house that held the offices of Carson, Andrews, and Szymanski, Attorneys at Law, she practically ran to the rear entrance, her boots sliding through crusty snow. Trevor stepped out from between the large juniper shrubs that flanked the sidewalk by the door. Corinne stopped, almost slipping as she covered her mouth to smother a scream. Trevor seized her arm, jerking her to face him.

"Good morning, baby," he said through clenched teeth.

"Let go of me, or I'll…"

"You'll what? Call the cops?" His strong fingers pressed deeper into her arm. She tried to pull away from his tightening grasp. "What do you think the cops will do when they hear about all the partying you did? They won't think you're much of a mother."

Corinne wrenched away finally, her eyes wide with fear. "That's a lie. You're the one who was partying."

"It's my word against yours. I'm concerned about my son. I want to make sure he's being well taken care of. You're unstable, maybe unfit. When they find your stash in the car, I'll get custody." His eyes narrowed, his voice was cruel. "Your old man isn't going to threaten me and get away with it."

"There's no stash in my car unless you put it there." She drew herself up and met his reptilian eyes with a steady gaze. The fear that had made her sick to her stomach melted away. Her voice was as solid as a deadbolt thrown through the latch. "My father was just protecting his grandson. Leave him out of this. You didn't want Keith, remember? You told me to get an abortion."

"Since you didn't, I have rights. Same as you."

"You had them, but you didn't want anything to do with either of us. I'm getting a restraining order against you today, and once my boss talks to the judge, there'll be a warrant for your arrest. They'll be very interested about the side business you had in New York. Prison is in your future, Trevor."

Trevor looked away and swallowed rapidly, his Adam's apple bobbing.

"It's still your word against mine." He began sliding back to the bushes. He scratched an unshaven cheek and stomped his feet, his breath visible in the cold.

"No. It's not. And I can prove it." She took a step forward. "Besides the drugs, you were and are a thief."

She willed herself to stand still and meet his gaze. This was a chance she had to take. "When I have the license plate run on that Jeep, they'll know for sure."

A rush of blood blotted Trevor's cheeks. He pushed past her, swearing and kicking up snow with his work boots. Corinne dashed into the building and went to find her boss. A half hour later, her gut instinct was confirmed. He was driving a stolen vehicle. She couldn't hesitate or back down now. Too much was at stake. It was time for Trevor to get his comeuppance, as her Grandpa Carroll would have said.

38

"They're both coming," Ruthanne related happily to Nan as they sat in Smokin' Joe's BBQ in Nairobi. It was brand new restaurant a few blocks from the school, and Nan rated the ribs and chicken as "not bad." The owner was an ex-patriot from Tennessee, who was bringing a taste of the American South to Kenya. Ruthanne had come to the city for her six-month checkup and a few days of R and R.

"Really? Both of them are able to come?" Nan asked as she picked up another rib and tore off a bite of smoky, sweet pork.

"The email came last night. It's all arranged. Dr. Hawkes is ecstatic to have another nurse for a whole month. We can do several immunization clinics and take care of some minor surgeries. We also have an orthopedic surgeon and a surgical nurse coming for two weeks in August. He's planning on several hip and knee surgeries. Beth is working with the mission. She'll be teaching classes on marriage, ministry leadership training for women, and some others. There's a group coming in August to dig a new well from Samaritan's Purse too. It's going to be a very busy month." Ruthanne was so excited that she felt like singing, but that would only annoy the other restaurant patrons since she couldn't carry a tune to save her life.

Nan grinned and dabbed a checkered napkin at the sauce from on her chin. "Quite a different vacation from the last time y'all were together."

Ruthanne sat back in the wooden chair and closed her eyes. "Much different. Even though Melody refuses to have anything to do with spiritual things, I sense a whole different attitude with her. We Skyped a couple of weeks ago. I've never seen her so happy—her job is going well. She graduated in the top three of her nursing class. Dale is a good guy. This trip might make all the difference."

"It could. You never know how Jesus is goin' to stir the pot in people's hearts. It's usually a messy process...ugh! Just like these dang ribs!" She laughed as she rubbed a glob of sauce from her yellow blouse. "And your checkup? How was that?"

Ruthanne shrugged. "About the same. They don't know why I'm still here."

"Are you OK then?"

"Of course."

"Are you fibbin' about this?" Nan tried to catch her friend's eyes.

Ruthanne looked up and smiled, looking her straight in the eye. "I'm dandy as candy," she responded with her best attempt at a Savannah drawl.

Nan raised her eyebrows skeptically, but Ruthanne was relieved to see that her report was taken at face value.

"I don't want to bring up a sore subject, but what about Audrey? Have you heard from her lately?"

Ruthanne shrugged and picked at the fruit salad on her plate.

"No. But that's all right. Leah emailed me that she and Rick had a good talk with Audrey at a fundraiser dinner a few months back. She was asking some questions about the mission even. Knowing Leah and Rick, they'll keep in touch with her. Oh, and she did email me at Christmas."

"That was six months ago," Nan exclaimed.

"It's all right. I have no right to expect anything more. I'm happy with the bit of correspondence we've had."

Ruthanne wished the statement was true. It was some days, but the hurt was still there underneath it all. A real relationship would be difficult anyway. Her life was here, and Audrey's was in New York. She prayed that Audrey would see her need for a Savior. The email she'd received from Audrey indicated that there was at least some interest in spiritual things. She'd even attended Leah's annual four-week Christmas Bible study. She could only pray that her daughter who was so self-sufficient, so independent, and so wealthy wouldn't be like the rich young ruler coming to Christ. He was too comfortable in his lifestyle to change. Oh, that the Lord Jesus would change her heart about what was truly important. Her eternity hung in the balance. Ruthanne's heart ached thinking about it. What if she didn't get to see Audrey in heaven, or for that matter, Melody? Her baby sister was in great spiritual need too. Her grudge with God and their long deceased father for a difficult childhood never seemed to wane.

It was odd how three girls growing up in the same home could take such different views of events and people. Daddy had been a complicated man, austere and sometimes harsh, but he had loved his family and served the church with everything he had. She remembered his late nights at the hospital, her mother wrapping up a casserole that he took to a needy church family. Then there was the endless procession of church life—weddings, funerals, baptisms, fellowship dinners, and so many more responsibilities that fall to pastors. In each of the five little churches he'd pastored over 30 years, the last one in Sheffield, the congregations had increased and ministries grown. It hadn't been an easy life, but one that had prepared her in many ways for Africa. She also remembered hearing her father's tearful prayers as he beseeched God Almighty to protect and bless his daughters. Ruthanne turned her attention back to the conversation.

"Well, you'll have your sisters here in eight weeks. Y'all will have a fabulous time if they're able to handle your primitive conditions down there. Girl, I don't know how you put up with some of that stuff."

"It's not for everybody, but I'm sure they'll manage," Ruthanne laughed. "On second thought—maybe. I'm optimistic, anyway."

Ruthanne knelt by her cot in the small guest room at the mission headquarters. So much whirled through her mind tonight. The joy of anticipating her sisters' arrival in just two months' time. Her test results weren't very good. The pain of knowing that some of the people she loved the most were so far away from God, separated from His forgiveness and salvation by their own choice. The continuing challenges of the school and the growing church that had spilled over into two more villages. Then there was the need for men to minister. They were so hard to reach with the gospel. Tradition and superstition were so ingrained in the Maasai culture. And then there was the poverty. Every once in a while, the problems seemed like the river near the village that overflowed its banks in the rainy season. There wasn't anything to contain the devastating muddy waters that swept livestock and sometimes people away to their deaths. She was just one person, with one meager sandbag against the flood.

Her Bible lay open on the bed to Paul's letter to the church at Philippi. She read through the verses of chapter four once more. They were long ago memorized, but she felt their renewed power as she read them aloud.

"Rejoice in the Lord always. I will say it again: Rejoice! Let your gentleness be evident to all. The Lord is

near. Do not be anxious about anything, but in everything by prayer and petition, with thanksgiving, present your requests to God. And the peace of God, which transcends all understanding, will guard your hearts and minds in Christ Jesus."

The evening prayer her father had taught her as a child flooded back in memory and then to her lips.

"Keep watch, dear Lord, with those who work or weep tonight, give your angels charge over us as we sleep. Comfort the sick, Lord Jesus, give us rest, bless the dying, soothe the suffering, give us joy in the morning; shelter us in your love. Amen."

39

Melody lugged her suitcases behind Beth as they plodded through the bustling Nairobi airport. Between delays and a missed connection, they were both exhausted. Melody dreamed of a hot shower and a comfortable bed. Her clothes were practically stiff since she'd been in them for two days straight. She strained to locate Nan, who was putting them up for the night. And then Nan was suddenly a few yards away, a gray-haired woman in a gloriously overstated purple and red sundress and Jackie O white-framed sunglasses. Their hostess was like a tall glass of icy lemonade to a bone-tired and sore traveler. She hoped Nan wasn't a mirage. Once clasped to Nan's generous bosom for an unforgettable hug, Melody was sure of reality.

The taxi ride to the school was another 20 minutes, which was like a never-ending amusement park ride. The driver had been tipped in advance to make sure they found the fastest route. Beth looked awfully queasy to Melody while Nan seemed to enjoy the entire jaunt, uttering encouragement in Swahili to the driver when he narrowly missed a flock of chickens. The old cab swerved fearlessly around bicycles, pedestrians, livestock, and buses. Melody closed her eyes, contemplating prayer for the first time in years. All that came to mind was "Now I lay me down to sleep" and "if I should die before I wake. . ."

Dinner, much to her relief, was a quiet affair in Nan's private quarters. She cooked a traditional Southern dinner with greens, fried chicken, candied sweet potatoes, and coconut cake for dessert. The rich, robust Kenyan coffee was the perfect complement to the cake, which they enjoyed on the verandah. The sounds of traffic and insects mingled with their conversation in the humid darkness. Melody hadn't been so excited about anything since starting nursing school. This adventure to the Maasai village and helping the people Ruthanne had dedicated her life to was especially meaningful.

She was pleasantly surprised at the relaxed conversations she'd enjoyed with Beth on the trip. It was quite different than the ones they'd had two years ago in Cape Cod. There was certainly less grist in the mill to grind between them. She wasn't sure if it was the change in Beth or herself. Maybe it was a combination. When they began to talk about Ruthanne, palpable sadness crept into the room.

"I was so sure we'd have this vacation all together," Melody started. "It's not really fair."

"I was too. She was doing so well, or at least, that's what we thought," Beth said.

"She was doing well for much longer than the doctors thought. I had a feelin' she wasn't exactly truthful with me in June. But I didn't want to press her." Nan poured herself another cup of coffee from the insulated carafe on the table.

"We need to visit her grave and say our goodbyes," Beth declared. "Everyone at the mission was so compassionate, but I need closure in seeing her home, the people she served, and...where she's buried." Beth sipped at her coffee and looked away.

"Ruthanne gave them all she had, and we can be proud of her. Everything must have happened quickly after the last set of tests," Melody struggled to control her emotions.

"Dr. Hawkes said it *was* very quick, when he was here," Nan assured them. "In many ways, that was a great blessin' for Ruthanne. Not to be languishin' in a hospital bed for months on end. That would have been the last thing Ruthanne could have borne."

"That's for sure." Melody found that her voice was a little steadier. "She'd be surprised at the change in Beth though. She has a lot to be proud of too."

Elizabeth blushed self-consciously. "A lot of hard work and getting out of my comfort zone mostly."

"A little simple on the explanation, Bethie," Melody teased. "She's lost 25 pounds and is a counselor at the women's shelter in Sheffield."

"Well done, Beth. I always admire those who can resist food. I have not, as you can see." Nan draped some of the generous yardage of the yellow and brown caftan over the arm of the chair for effect. "Elastic and caftans are a girl's best friends. Tell me what you're doin' at that shelter."

Beth explained that she was teaching abused women about childcare, budgeting, and homemaking skills. It was a long way from teaching a women's Sunday School class and serving on the Mission Committee.

"I've learned a lot over the last two years. I have so much to be thankful for and nothing to complain about. In fact I memorized Philippians 2:14 right away when I began working there." Beth recited:

"Do everything without complaining and arguing."

She sighed. "I've had to let go of a lot of complaining and control issues. God is faithful, and He is in control. I just need to let Him be in control."

"Ah, and therein lies the rub," Nan chuckled. "We do like to control it all, but it's totally impossible. We forget He's the only one who can really see the big picture. Africa reminds you of that fact every day without fail."

For Melody, the conversation had already fallen into an uncomfortable religious theme. "I *really* need to get some sleep," she announced. "I think Dr. Hawkes has a pretty rigorous schedule planned for me." She stretched her arms overhead, uttering a small groan.

Nan smiled. "That is also a fact. The good doctor was here a couple of weeks ago pickin' up supplies. He's very anxious for you to arrive."

Beth gave in to a wide yawn. "I'm sorry, but two days in airports and the time changes have caught up with me."

"Amen, sister," Melody mirrored the yawn, placing her dessert plate on the table next to her coffee cup. "We have a long day ahead of us tomorrow to get to Ruthanne's village."

"If y'all get a good night's sleep tonight, you'll be on African time in a flash. It's quite a trek, so y'all need a good eight hours. Might not get much after that," Nan said.

Elizabeth and Melody jounced along in the back seat of the Land Rover, dust caking their arms and legs. There was no air-conditioning in the vehicle, but the driver was a decided change of pace from the taxi driver of the previous afternoon. Dr. Muhs, who sat next to the driver, commented little on the exotic terrain. He had longish brown hair pulled back in a short ponytail. He wore black-framed glasses that gave him the appearance of age, but Melody had agreed with Beth that the doctor had to be less than forty. He seemed reticent to join the lively conversation with the driver, who happily explained flora and fauna.

They stopped for lunch in a shady grove of acacia trees. Melody and Beth had their cameras in action, snapping at everything in sight. The vistas were amazing in Rift Valley. The sky was a huge expanse of sapphire and opalescent clouds, the mountains stately and green, and the wildlife plentiful. So far, they had seen herds of gazelle, a rhino, a herd of wildebeests, eagles, and a pair of skulking hyenas. The driver assured them that the possibility of seeing a lion or two lay ahead of them. In another hour, they should be at their destination. Dr. Muhs stared through his binoculars toward the mountains to the east of the single-lane dirt road.

"I can totally understand why Ruthanne loved it here," Melody chirped. "It's incredible! And hot!" She rubbed trickling sweat from her forehead with the back of her hand.

"It's really beyond words—all of this." Beth swept her arms around. She'd never seen such wild beauty. "It's breathtaking! Have you been to Kenya before, Dr. Muhs?"

"No. This is my first time," he responded, concentrating on the sandwich he'd pulled from the large ice chest the driver had hauled from the Land Rover. Both women grabbed bottles of water eagerly from its icy depths.

"So, what do you think of all this?" Melody pressed him. She took a swig of water and rolled the bottle against her neck.

"Very nice."

"Nice? Really?" Melody's voice was sharp. Beth cleared her throat to catch her sister's attention. It would be a long four weeks if Mel alienated Dr. Muhs before they even reached their destination.

"Overpowering and wild is more accurate. Would you like me to take your picture together here?" The doctor smiled and nodded his head in the direction of a large tree. The vista spread out beyond it like a richly textured tapestry of greens, blues, browns, and golds.

Beth nodded, appreciative of the doctor's smooth diversionary tactic. She looked at Melody, who shrugged. "Sure, why not?"

Their driver Manny honked the horn as they wheeled into the village in a cloud of dust. A crowd of boys and girls rushed the vehicle, singing what Beth thought was a Maasai version of *Jesus Loves Me*, but she wasn't sure. A tall, dark-haired man in a white short-sleeved shirt and khaki shorts strode through the confusion, his hand extended to Melody.

"You must be Mrs. Mucher," he said, helping her from the Land Rover. "And you must be Mrs. Hartman. Dr. Muhs, I presume," he chuckled at his own bad joke, extending a hand to the hesitant surgeon. "I'm Eric Hawkes. Welcome to Maasai Land. My nurse, Carolyn Spear, will show you to the clinic and your quarters, doctor."

A middle-aged woman with salt and pepper hair, dressed in a yellow abstract print blouse and jeans, motioned for Dr. Muhs to follow her.

"Thank you for meeting us," Beth said, brushing layers of dust from her Bermudas and blouse. If it was this thick on her clothes, she was going to need a long hot shower. How had Ruthanne stood all of the dust? And was there a shower of any kind here?

"My pleasure," said Dr. Hawkes. "It's least I can do. Let me show you to your living quarters."

Beth stood, momentarily frozen at the scene around her, assorted children, along with tall, elegant women, dressed in bright colors and intricately beaded hair, babies on their hips. The smell of manure and lowing cattle in the distance made her think of an uncle's farm where, as children, the three sisters drank warm fresh milk from a shared tin cup in the milkhouse. Chickens ran around the loaf-shaped huts, which she knew were called *inkajijik*, according to Ruthanne. The *kraal* that surrounded the village of 40 or more huts was sturdy and wicked looking, with the sharp thorns of the acacia woven and stacked to keep lions and other predators out.

She hoped that she wouldn't be asked to drink blood or anything mixed with blood. That wasn't something she could handle. The Maasai were historically a nomadic warrior tribe where blood and beef were the staples. Western influence had eroded the independent culture of these tall, proud people, who were now tilling gardens and roaming very little. Their poverty was extreme. She could see that her sister had not exaggerated about the conditions. They were stunningly awful, and she knew the work here would be hard. Beth turned to see Dr. Hawkes and Melody heading to a large, whitewashed cement block building that must be the school. Patting a few children's heads, she hurried to catch up. The trio stopped to read the sign by the front door.

Dedicated to Ruthanne Carroll

Warrior for Jesus and the Maasai

We wait in hope for the LORD; he is our help

and our shield. Psalm 33:20

"What will the school do now that Ruthanne is gone?" Beth asked. Her voice trembled as she stared at the sign. She brushed back tears with her hand. She would allow herself to cry later—in private. Melody blew her nose, tears running down her face.

"That prayer was answered two weeks before Ruthanne died," he said slowly, running his hand along the top of the engraved metal sign. "The days she spent in the infirmary were not idle. She prayed day and night that they would find a replacement for her. Steve Kauffman, the mission director, was pretty concerned about finding the right person. He and his wife couldn't do it. They had too many other responsibilities, and they were due to go on furlough, which they needed after the school project. Two people had turned it down. But the Lord delivered an interim principal just in time. She's here for six months, which will give the mission some additional time to find a permanent replacement. The real blessing was that Ruthanne spent her last three days with the interim, which really eased her mind.

You'll be sharing the school's apartment with her. Don't worry, it has two bedrooms," he added quickly.

Beth wished her hesitation hadn't been so evident on her face. She and Mel hadn't known what their living arrangements would be, and a new apartment would be miles better than anything she could see around it.

"Steve added this nice apartment at the rear of the school. I think you'll find it much more comfortable than the *inkajijik* Ruthanne lived in all those years. She did enjoy real luxury here for almost a year, which helped her a great deal healthwise when she came back from the States. Some extra funds came in and furnished the apartment, which was an added bonus."

He led them to the rear of the long, red metal-roofed building. He knocked on the heavy wooden door, which was opened quickly by a Maasai woman.

"Hellen," Dr. Hawkes said, "this is Beth and Melody—Miss Ruth's sisters."

The tall, thin woman, who wore a deep red dress tied with black and white sash, smiled broadly and clapped her hands, motioning them to enter.

"Hellen was Ruthanne's housekeeper for many years," he explained.

"Yes, right," Beth recalled. "Ruthanne spoke of Hellen often. It's so good to meet you."

"Welcome, welcome! I am so happy to meet the beautiful sisters of our beautiful Miss Ruth."

After hugs were exchanged they followed Hellen into the coolness of the small living area that was set for tea.

Beth noticed that the china was Royal Albert's *Autumn Roses*, which was Grandma Erickson's china pattern.

"What gorgeous china," she exclaimed. "Was this Ruthanne's?"

"No. It's mine, and I'm surprised it made the trip," called a woman's voice from the kitchen. A slender, young woman carried a plate of fruit and set it on the low table in front of the rough-hewn sofa. She wore blue linen cropped pants and a white tank top. Ropes of colorful beads hung around her neck. Her short hair was dark with blond highlights framing her face. Her eyes were a startling gray and her smile contagious. It was obvious Dr. Hawkes was captivated. He followed the woman's every move. Beth could understand his fascination. She was an attractive woman.

"I'm Audrey Wright," she said, offering a hand. "What a pleasure to meet my aunts."

Beth gasped and sat down on the sofa, rattling the delicate china. Melody took the offered hand and laughed.

The Time Under Heaven

There is a time for everything,
A season for every activity under heaven.
A time to be born and a time to die.
A time to plant and a time to harvest.
A time to kill and a time to heal.
A time to tear down and a time to rebuild.
A time to cry and a time to laugh.
A time to grieve and a time to dance.
A time to scatter stones and a time to gather stones.
A time to embrace and a time to turn away.
A time to search and a time to lose.
A time to keep and a time to throw away.
A time to tear and a time to mend.
A time to be quiet and a time to speak up.
A time to love and a time to hate.
A time for war and a time for peace.

Ecclesiastes 3:1-8 NLT

21767492R00151

Made in the USA
Charleston, SC
29 August 2013